DIRTY GIRL

GIRL

Book One of the The Dirty Girl Duet

Meghan March

ABOUT THIS BOOK

DESPERATELY SEEKING RICH, FAMOUS, SINGLE GUY
WITH A GIANT COCK TO MAKE MY LYING, CHEATING,
SHOULD'VE-BEEN-BORN-DICKLESS EX-BOYFRIEND
REALIZE WHAT HE'S JUST LOST.
OH, AND I GIVE GREAT HEAD. JUST SAYIN'.

No man in his right mind would answer that ad.

Except thousands did.

My name is Greer Karas, and I should never be allowed near another bottle of booze again. Because when I drink, my friend and I do stupid things. Like take a page out of my older brother's playbook and post something completely asinine on the Internet. Waking up with a giant hangover to find my humiliating personal ad has gone viral is not my finest moment.

Cue my look of shock when one of Hollywood's hottest new bad boys, Cavanaugh Westman, comes knocking at my door and drops his pants to prove that he does indeed have a giant cock.

What he doesn't have is an explanation for why he disappeared from my life without a word three years ago, only to show up on the big screen two years later, killing bad guys in action flicks.

He wants me again.

What the hell do I do now?

CHAPTER
ONE

Greer

Have you ever done something you know is a bad idea, but you're being egged on by your best friend, and the heat of liquor pooling in your belly destroys any concern about potential consequences? Yeah, I did that last night, and a hangover isn't the only thing I'm regretting. Oh no, I'm a *go big or go home* kind of girl. I should have gone home.

"Oh my God, B, you gotta undo it. Shit. Shit. Shit. I'll get fired over this!" Panic permeates my words as I jam my hands into my snarl of post-blackout-drunk hair.

My best friend, Banner, named by her übergenius geek of a father for the legendary comic book character Bruce Banner, tilts her head to the side as she studies her phone's screen. With a wince, she looks up.

I already know what she's going to say before she

opens her mouth. I'm so screwed.

"I'm sorry, babe, but it's not undoable. It's pretty much the opposite of undoable at this point. They call it viral for a reason. Even if I delete it from the site, it's already been shared thousands of times."

I slump into the couch, my body going boneless. "Fuck my life." I groan, throwing an arm over my eyes as if that will help shield me from the consequences of my poor judgment.

"Have you checked your e-mail?"

I peek out from under my arm to look at her, like a little kid who watches a horror movie from between spread fingers over her eyes in hopes of being less terrified in smaller doses. My brain is still chugging along at hangover speed, so I don't quite understand where she's going with this question.

"Checked for an e-mail from my very snooty, very white-shoe law firm informing me that my employment as an associate attorney has been terminated? No. No, I have not." Normally I monitor my work e-mail religiously, but right now I'm too chicken to open it.

Banner lays her phone facedown on the gray coffee table between us. "Not that account," she says, turning and tucking one leg under her on the couch. "The one we set up for the other e-mails. Oh, and don't forget the direct messages on Twitter."

My memories of last night may be a little fuzzy, but there are certain things that stand out in vivid Technicolor. Like coming up with a ridiculous password for the e-mail account GreerOneBadBitchKaras@rockyourface.

com, and my new Twitter account with the same handle. I shove my arm back over the slit of my vision.

Jeeeeezus. Hot mess alert. And on that note, I'm so terribly sorry, alcohol, but we need to break up.

I inject some optimism, or maybe just naïveté, into my tone. "No one would really respond to that ad, would they? I mean, it was clearly a joke."

Banner tugs my arm away from my face and squeezes my hand. I'd like to say it's a squeeze in solidarity, but it's probably more along the lines of a *you're my best friend and we both know you're totally fucked* squeeze.

She delivers her words patiently, the way you'd talk to a toddler who doesn't quite understand actual words yet. "Greer, we used your name. Being that you are who you are, what in God's name makes you think that people wouldn't respond?"

Snatching my hand back, I jam the heels of my palms into my eyes. "Can't you just lie to me? I'm trying to find some way to turn back time so my life isn't so epically screwed."

"Sorry, babe. Ain't happening. You were pretty adamant about it last night, and I wasn't about to contradict you." Banner pushes off the couch, and I hope she's going to get a tranquilizer to put me out of my misery.

No such luck. She crosses to the granite kitchen island and grabs my tablet. Her fingernails are tapping away on the screen when she asks, "What was the password again?"

She waits until I mumble something incoherent in response.

"Come again?"

I stare at the deep purple nail polish that's chipping on my thumbnail. Why can't my life be fixed as easily as my manicure? Oh, that's right, because life isn't for the faint of heart.

"Greer?"

I look up, mentally begging her to drop it. Do we really need to know the extent of my humiliation? I slap my hands down on the velvet sectional cushions on either side of me.

"This is pointless. Even if some whack jobs respond, I'm just going to ignore them and block their e-mails. There's no point in checking."

Banner glares at me. "Password."

Given that I've known her since prep school, I know she won't stop until I cave.

"Ionlysuckbigcocks69." It comes out on a single breath in a new dialect of the language *mumble*.

When a crooked smile lit with pure amusement spreads across Banner's face, I grab a toss pillow off the sectional and fling it at her head.

"Bitch. You already knew!"

"I had to hear you say it out loud. Because it's fan-frig-ging-tastic. I might change all my passwords today. They're clearly not creative enough. It's like an anthem for women everywhere."

I scan the area around me for additional projectiles, but come up empty. *Why don't I have more knickknacks?*

"It's not like I came up with it all by myself," I remind her.

She was just as drunk last night while we laughed over

the ad, the personal ad I placed *in my real name* in the crazy hopes that one particular guy would see it. A guy who clearly wasn't interested in me before and isn't now either.

He's known where to find me for years. It wasn't until a year ago that I finally figured out where he was.

How messed up is it to go to a movie with your friends and see the guy you had a mad crush on displayed center screen during the previews? The guy who broke your barely twenty-something-year-old heart before you could even get to the naked fun times?

Cavanaugh Westman, Hollywood's newest bad boy. It didn't matter that he'd changed, gotten bigger and more dangerous looking. I'd know him anywhere. Shaggy brown hair, curling just over his collar, hazel eyes that you could never predict the color of—anywhere from green to grayish-blue or tawny brown. It didn't shock me that Hollywood agents had apparently fallen in love with him. His body was ridiculous. Thick, sculpted muscles covered with inked, bronzed skin—

"Holy. Shit. No. Way."

Banner's low words drag me from my little trip down memory lane, and I jerk my head in her direction.

"What?"

She holds up the iPad and I shove to my feet, leaving the safety of my cozy couch to join her.

"You've got over five thousand new e-mails. And somehow, almost a half million new followers on Twitter, thanks to last night. Color you popular, lady."

My stomach bottoms out before twisting into a sickly, complicated knot as I take the tablet from her. "Oh. My.

God." My phone vibrates across the kitchen island before I can even begin to read.

My attention snaps to my phone as I dread who might be calling. There are two possibilities, both daunting but one more so: The chair of the professional staff committee from my firm calling to deliver my termination notice. Or worse, my brother.

I shove the iPad back into Banner's hands and snatch up the phone to check the display. *Crey.*

"Shit."

"Is it your brother?" she asks, knowing Creighton well enough from my birthdays and other events over the years.

"Yep."

"Well, it's not like he can say much. He practically invented the scandalous viral ad."

That's the truth, but it doesn't mean my brother would want to exchange stories of how we found our respective ways into the gossip rags by posting moronic things online.

No, he won't find the humor in how much his little sis follows in his footsteps. First, he'll want to kill my ex-boyfriend, Tristan—who he never liked anyway, and then, he's probably going to hire me a babysitter in addition to the bodyguard he forced on me last year. We toned down the security a few months back when I threatened to move out of the country to get away from him. Now I only have a driver who ferries me to and from work and anywhere else I need to go. I don't traipse the streets of New York by myself anymore, especially not late at night.

Holding my phone as it continues to vibrate, I debate how big my lady balls are today. *Not so very big.*

I let it go to voice mail. Nothing good can come of answering it. I'm too old to be scolded like an errant child, but I have a feeling Creighton won't agree with that assessment.

Instead, I round the couch to sink back into the safety of its plush cushions. Banner plops down beside me as I slide my phone next to hers on the table. She sets up my tablet facing us both, the list of e-mails mocking me with their subject lines like:

I'LL MAKE YOU MY BAD BITCH

MY COCK WILL ROCK YOUR WORLD

SEND ME A PICTURE OF YOUR FEET

The last one sends a creeper-worthy shiver of disgust down my spine. Apparently my viral ad brings out all the freak shows.

At a time like this, I could use the guidance of my big brother, but I know I've fucked up too badly to ask. Humiliation isn't something I deal with well.

Curling into a ball, I wrap my arms around my legging-clad knees. "What the hell am I going to do now?"

Banner's slouchy sweatshirt slips down over her shoulder, and she tugs it up before shrugging and offering her sage advice.

"There's really only one thing you can do—ride the wave of notoriety for all it's worth. Who knows, you might actually get a rich, hot, famous guy who's hung like a horse. And then you'll fuck your way into the sunset and live happily ever after with a big cock in your bed every night."

I toss my arm over my eyes again and groan. *I'm so fucked.* And not in the way Banner is hoping.

CHAPTER TWO

Cav

"Fuck you, Westman. I think you broke my god-damned face!"

I didn't, but Peyton DeLong is a pussy who would think a bitch slap hurts. If I had tried to break his face, he'd be on his way to the ER right now instead of crying over a bloody nose.

I'm not supposed to be throwing real punches on the set anymore, but sometimes a man's gotta make an exception. I haven't heard her name in over a year, and I'll be damned if I'll let this prick run it through the mud.

"Then keep your mouth shut and learn some fucking manners." I pitch my voice low, letting a growl invade, and I'm surprised DeLong doesn't piss himself where he stands.

Hollywood assholes. They don't know shit about real

life. And I'm one of them now. I stop myself from hanging my head at how far my life has veered off the path I thought it would take.

Mitch Stark, the director who pushed me to make the jump from stuntman to legit actor, strides over.

"If you two can't figure out a way to get through this without another pissing match, I will rain down hell like you've never experienced. You won't be able to buy yourself a decent role when I'm done blackballing you."

"He started it."

My fists ache to shut down DeLong's whine. Those veneers won't look so perfect scattered on the ground.

The only reason I accepted this role was because of Mitch. DeLong had been an unwelcome late addition to the cast, and I'll eat Spam and live in my car on skid row before I'll ever do another film with him.

"I'm done here." Without wasting another second of brainpower on DeLong, I stride in the direction of my trailer.

"You walking away from me, boy?"

Mitch is one of only two men I'll let speak to me that way. For a guy on the downhill side of sixty, he's got some speed in his gait as he tails me down the dusty path.

Good. Means I don't need to slow down.

"Thought you were done leveling threats, old man."

The slicing power of his arctic glare would make many an actor blank on a line or blow a cue, but I refuse to fear him. He stomps up the stairs behind me, the aluminum door slapping against the side of the trailer before it slams shut with us both inside.

"You ever going to lose that chip on your shoulder?" Mitch asks, crossing his arms over his chest. Even at his age, he's still got power in those muscles, and right now he looks like he wants to take me out back and beat some sense into me. Not a chance in hell, regardless of how much I respect him.

"Probably not." My answer is surprisingly honest.

"Shame, because any other director would toss you off the set and fine you for what you just did."

I raise my chin, that chip on my shoulder fueling my response. "Then fine me."

His steely blue gaze bores into me. "I would if I thought it would make a damn difference."

He's right. It won't.

"What do you want from me, Mitch?" I cross my arms over my chest.

"How about an explanation about what set that shit off? You don't want a reputation as a loose cannon, Cav. It'll kill your career so fast, you won't know what happened."

While I might not have wanted to be Hollywood's hottest new action star, I'm not ready to give it up either. I'm hooked. Not only on the challenge of it, but being part of creating something that allows millions of people to escape from their lives for a few hours at a time.

I spent plenty of hours trying to escape my childhood reality holed up in a ratty movie theater watching larger-than-life heroes take on the bad guys. The thought of giving that same escape to a kid like me is more than enough to keep me going, and that's only part of my motivation.

Although at that age, I wondered why bad guys in movies didn't win like they did in real life. Some lessons are learned early and often.

"Cav, you gonna give me something here or am I talking to myself?"

I yank open the mini fridge door and snag two bottles of water. Wishing they were beer doesn't replace the cans I crushed last night.

Almost done with this fucking movie, I remind myself. *Then I don't ever have to work with DeLong again.*

I toss one to Mitch and twist the cap off the other before lowering myself into a recliner.

"I wasn't talking about a bottle of water, kid."

Mitch won't let this go until he has some sort of explanation. I can bullshit him, but instead I go with the truth out of respect.

"He was runnin' his mouth about a woman."

The old man sinks onto the kitchenette bench, drops the bottle of water onto the table, and runs a hand through his thinning gray hair. "For fuck's sake, Cav. A piece of tail ain't worth your reputation."

That's where he's wrong. Especially when she's a hell of a lot more than a piece of tail.

"It's a long story." I want him to drop it and save me from getting sucked any deeper into the life I left behind.

"Enlighten me." The steel in his gaze has made its way into his voice, but I don't follow orders any more.

"Not important." A lie. Because it's damn important to me.

"Important enough to put your career at risk. Come

on, kid. Spill. Maybe I can help before you make this into a bigger mess."

Mitch is the only guy I've met in this business who has ever made me an offer of help, expecting nothing in return. That's not something I can buy, and the knowledge pushes me to loosen my tight grip on my secrets.

"There's a girl I was hung up on back in the day. She put herself front and center in the news, and DeLong was looking to cash in on what he considers an easy score." Little does DeLong know, nothing about Greer Karas is easy.

Mitch cranks open his bottle of water, his eyes never leaving mine as he sucks half of it down. He replaces the cap, his brain working over everything I've told him before he finally speaks.

"Is this going to be a problem?"

I follow his lead, drinking and considering before I answer.

"I think DeLong got the message loud and clear."

Mitch lays an arm on the kitchenette table and leans forward. "Fuck DeLong. Is this a problem for you? Because we've got two days to wrap this project so I can start my vacation."

Mitch's daughter is taking him to Italy for some relaxation over his birthday. No one on this set will let filming slip even a day because no one wants to be responsible for fucking that up for him. Me included. Even when all I want to do is get on a jet and get my ass back to New York so I can shake some sense into that girl.

"No, man. My head's in the game. I've only got the one scene left, and I'm done. I ain't holding up shit."

"You sure? Because you're goddamn lucky I don't need Peyton's face anymore."

A twinge of guilt slips into my chest. I didn't even consider whether Mitch did or not before I popped DeLong in the nose with a jab. He's lucky I didn't swing with a right hook, or he would have a broken face for sure.

Mitch waits for an answer, his attention fixed on me.

"I'm sure."

"Good." He pushes to his feet. "If that shit happens again on one of my projects, I'll make you wish you'd never stepped foot in Hollywood, regardless of how much I like you."

I say nothing as he turns and shoulders open the trailer door, letting it bang shut behind him as he mutters to himself.

"Fucking kids these days . . ."

Mitch is old guard, from a dying breed of directors. I know I'm lucky to have a chance to work with him, not just on this film but the first one he used to drag me into this business and out of being a glorified crash-test dummy. Disappointing him wasn't on my schedule for today, but the guilt remains regardless.

Slumping against the back of the recliner, I fish my phone out of my pocket. I don't know why I pull it up again, but I can't help it.

What the fuck were you thinking, Greer? God, but I want to shake that girl. She's not the slutty little princess this ad makes her out to be.

I read through it again, stumbling over the part about her giving great head. I wouldn't know. We hadn't made it that far, no matter how badly I wanted her lips wrapped around my cock back then.

Screw shaking her—I want to take her over my knee and turn that luscious ass red. She's begging to be taken in hand, and in my gut, I know this ad was a direct shot aimed at me.

Greer Karas, sister of the legendary billionaire Creighton Karas, has no idea how effective that shot is.

My cock pulses against my jeans when I think of her on her knees, her pouty lips wrapped around my dick as I teach her how to swallow it down. Greer might think she knows how to give good head, but I'm not one of the trust fund kids she's used to.

Three years ago, I knew she needed a man to keep her out of trouble. Seems that some things haven't changed. As soon as this project is wrapped, I'll be on that jet to New York, and Greer Karas and I are going to get reacquainted. Intimately.

Three years ago, I walked before I could dirty up her pristine little world. But now? All bets are off.

CHAPTER
THREE

Greer

I step off East 53rd into the building that houses Sterling & Michaels, and I swear even the security guards are looking at me funny. It shouldn't be a surprise. I'm an Internet sensation.

Creighton kept me out of the press for years, but even he won't be able to bury this disaster, which I'm sure he's trying to do, even though I keep letting his calls go to voice mail. By its very nature, something viral can't be undone. My brother knows that as well as anyone.

There's no choice but to brazen it out as I stride across the gray and white marble floor in my most conservative pinstriped skirt suit with my heels clicking with every step. I might not be able to hold on to my job, but I will maintain my dignity at any cost.

When I swipe my badge at the turnstile, it flashes

green, admitting me to the elevator bank. Surprise and optimism fill me because if I were fired, I wouldn't even be able to get up to my office. It's a highly effective measure for not having to deal with people you don't want to deal with.

The elevator seems even more painfully slow than normal as it climbs to the forty-seventh floor, allowing me too much time to play out the scenarios in my brain. *I'm so screwed.*

The cherrywood-paneled walls with brushed gold lettering greet me as I step out with faux confidence, holding my chin high. The receptionist's automatic smile falters once she realizes who I am.

Her name is Jade, and she started here the same day I did. We share the same birthday, the same love of Holly Wix and Boone Thrasher's country music, and under different circumstances, I could be her. She's going to college at night while she works here during the day, and raises a toddler alone after her boyfriend bailed without a word or a dime.

I tried to talk her into letting me use Creighton's PI to track down his sorry ass so she could get child support, but Jade freaked when I suggested it. She claims having him out of their lives is for the best, even if she's struggling to stretch every paycheck to make ends meet.

Jade glances from side to side to confirm the lobby is empty, and I can feel the come-to-Jesus speech in the air before she speaks the first word.

"Seriously, G, what the hell were you thinking? Are you trying to get fired?"

In that moment, guilt washes over me. Jade would kill to have my job, and here I am, recklessly endangering it because I decided finding the bottom of a fifth of gin with Banner was a solid idea for getting over the sight of my boyfriend pumping into a skinny redhead's ass.

I blurt out the first thought in my brain. "He didn't even stop fucking her to chase after me."

Jade's eyes widen in confusion. "What are you talking about?"

"Tristan."

Understanding dawns over her features, and her hands fist defensively. "Shit. I should have known this had something to do with that little fucker."

Not quite over the raunchy humor Banner and I were indulging in all night, I respond honestly. "He definitely was little. In every way."

Jade stands behind the cherry desk and leans forward. "Why didn't you call me to help hide the body?" Her voice is low and serious.

Mentioning that my brother's secret mob connection might have been a better option had I gone that route might not be the best choice at this particular moment. Anyway, I wasn't moved to violence last night. Instead, after the shock of seeing my boyfriend of two years nailing another woman passed, a hollow sort of emptiness took up residence in my chest, along with the gaping pit of failure.

"Greer. You there?"

My attention snapped back to Jade. "Sorry, I left him alive. No hazmat suits needed."

"Well, maybe you should've called me before you decided to get shit-faced, because that's the only way I can see you posting that ad. What were you thinking? Gah. Why didn't you call me? I would've been there to hand you booze, food, and veto your Internet privileges."

Her words fire the first real smile to grace my lips today. "Next time I catch my boyfriend fucking another chick, I'll call you first."

Her scowl intensifies. "I would've killed him."

"Sometimes killing people isn't the right answer."

The elevator opens behind me with a ding and I freeze, not wanting to turn around and see who it is.

Kevin Sunderberg's nasally voice gives his pompous identity away, saving me the hassle of worrying for more than a hot second.

"I can't believe you'd even show your face here, Karas. That takes serious balls. Which apparently you're well acquainted with." Under his breath, he whispers, "Slut."

I don't need to see him to picture his acne-scarred face twisted with disgust.

Jade stiffens in her chair but I hold out a hand, signaling her to stand down. She's made an art form out of ignoring the comments of the assholes who work in this place when they're directed at her, but she's more than ready to come to my defense.

I won't let her get fired because of me, though. I can handle Sunderberg myself.

He's hated me since our third year of law school when I wrecked the curve in Corporate Finance. As a result, he lost his perfect GPA and his spot as first in our class. I graduated third in the class to his second, but he's never gotten over it. Or maybe it's the fact that I turned down his drunken passes at a bar a couple of months before graduation.

I turn to face him. His blond hair is already thinning on top, and I'm guessing he's going to opt for the combover before he's thirty.

"It's better than being a wannabe manwhore like you, Kevin." The burn isn't as good as I'd like, but I'm off my game today.

"You come in here to get your ass chewed out in person?" His words are laced with loathing. "I would say fired, but we both know they won't dare. It's such a fucking joke. Any other associate would be out on her ass for doing what you did, embarrassing the shit out of yourself and the firm. But no, not the untouchable Greer Karas. They wouldn't dare fire you and risk losing your brother's business."

There are several things I truly despise, and one of them is admitting Kevin Sunderberg is right. When I let my rational brain take the lead, I know my fears about getting fired are probably unfounded. Realistically, I *am* virtually untouchable here. The firm makes millions from the litigation it handles for Karas International. My brother is not a man others want to anger.

"I suggest you worry about yourself and the hours you need to bill today."

His lip curls like he's just eaten bad sushi. "You're a joke, Greer." He spins on his Prada loafers and heads for the internal staircase.

"And so is his dick."

Jade's hushed voice comes from behind me, and I swing around to stare at her, distracted momentarily from Kevin's harsh words.

"You've seen his dick?"

She drops her gaze to the desktop in front of her. "Not my proudest moment. But I was desperate and he had a penis. Arguably."

A giggle spills from my lips at the comic relief I desperately need at this moment. "Really, Jade? *Really*?"

Jade's dimples appear as she fights her own laugh. "Let's just say the size requirement in your ad was probably the smartest part of the whole debacle."

My humor dies mid-giggle and I groan, covering my face with my hand. When I look back at her, her expression is sober once more.

"I should get fired today. Kevin's right."

Jade shrugs. "Fuck 'em. If they don't have the balls to fire you, then that's their problem. Not yours."

As much as I appreciate her practical attitude, I know it will become my problem. It doesn't take working in a firm very long to realize lawyers aren't nearly as confrontational as people expect. Passive-aggressive bullshit will be heaped on me in the form of terrible projects, midnight conference calls with Asia, and deadlines requiring all-nighters.

I always thought I would love my job. I was wrong. *So, what is the point of sticking it out if I know what abuse is coming?*

I came to the office today to apologize and beg forgiveness, to try to salvage my career, and all it took was Kevin Sunderberg's venom to make me form a completely different plan.

Jade's right. Fuck 'em. I'll find another job, and I won't go crawling to my brother for one either.

With the knowledge that my self-respect won't be sacrificed on the altar of Sterling & Michaels today, my spine finds new reinforcement. "Okay. Wish me luck."

Jade's perfectly sculpted eyebrows draw together. "What are you going to do?"

"Nothing good for my career."

CHAPTER FOUR

Greer

I lug the box of my personal belongings through the lobby and hand over my badge to security.

"Thanks, Donald."

"Anytime, Ms. Karas."

His words are the throwaway kind because we both know there won't be another time. I'm done with Sterling & Michaels.

My bright, shiny career as an associate came to a crashing halt when I handed Mr. Feinstein the letter of resignation I'd typed in my office thirty minutes ago. His insincere attempt to change my mind was less than impressive, as was his request that I explain to my brother that my decision was neither prompted nor supported by the firm.

I stopped by Kevin Sunderberg's office on my way out

and dropped an armload of deal toys on his desk. He's always wanted the little trophies representing the hundreds of thankless hours I worked helping clients buy and sell companies. *He's welcome to them. I'm done.*

With a final glance over my shoulder, I step out onto East 53rd, wondering if anyone is going to come chasing after me to snatch back the pro bono file I'd lifted from my filing cabinet. It's the only client file I grabbed on my way out. Chances are no one will miss it.

I've been working on this prisoners' rights case here and there for a couple of months with little progress. Two phone interviews with an inmate at Rikers Island about the impingement of his constitutional rights and a crime he says he didn't commit.

Why would a corporate associate attorney handle a prisoners' rights case pro bono? Welcome to the wonderful world of giving back in the legal community. You don't even have to be qualified to handle a case, just willing to give it a shot. Most associates try to dodge these assignments for all they're worth, but I actually volunteered for this one. It's the one project I worked on that didn't directly pad someone else's bottom line.

Maybe this is my penance. I can get some kind of justice for this guy, and it'll give me something to do while I figure out my next step.

Ed, my driver, pulls up at the curb as I heft the box higher in my arms. He exits the car and comes around to the side to snatch it from my grip.

"Ms. Karas, you should have notified me in your text that I needed to retrieve something from your office."

"No worries, Ed. I managed."

There's no way in hell I wanted him to see the looks that followed me as I made my walk of shame out of the office. Kevin Sunderberg had made sure to fake cough *whore* loud enough for everyone on the floor to hear it. *Unoriginal prick.*

"Home, then?"

"Yes. Thank you." I slide inside the Mercedes, acknowledging silently that I have absolutely no idea what I'm going to do next.

My phone buzzes again. *Crey.*

I should answer. Should explain everything and tell him I've quit my job, but I don't want to do it. He's always been so proud of me, and right now, there's nothing to be proud of. I'm a fuckup. Such a cliché.

The call goes to voice mail, and Ed's phone rings.

"Yes, sir. One moment, sir."

He looks in the rearview mirror and holds out the phone. Ed doesn't need to say anything because I already know who it is. I want to take the phone and hang up, but even I'm not capable of being that childish. I can't run from Creighton forever.

I hold Ed's phone to my ear. "Hi."

"What the fuck are you doing, Greer?" His voice is harsh in my ear, and my wince is automatic.

Yes, I'm a fuckup.

"Hello to you too, Crey." I try to brazen my way out of it.

"When I call, I expect you to fucking answer."

Bristling against the back of the leather seat, I inject

attitude into my tone. "I don't work for you, Crey, so don't you dare talk to me like that."

I hear something through the phone, the sound of him growling?

"Women. So fucking stubborn."

"Say hello to Holly for me."

"Stop with the bullshit, Greer. What the fuck were you thinking? Did you even think at all? And that ad . . . why the hell would you do that? I've got PR working their asses off, and we can't stop the spread. At this point, the only people who haven't seen it are in fucking North Korea and maybe China."

"I know," I say quietly as shame crashes down around me. I feel like a child again, being taken to task on the rug in front of my uncle's desk.

"Jesus, Greer. Do you realize what's happening to the stock of the companies?"

His words hit me like a fist to the gut. "Why would that matter?"

"Because your trust is a goddamn majority shareholder in a bunch of them. But no, you didn't think about the kind of monetary impact your actions could have before you posted that asinine ad making you look like a—" He breaks off before he can deliver the final blow.

"Just say it, Crey. Like a whore? A slut? Jesus, this fucking double-standard stuff is bullshit. You posted something just as ridiculous and probably *made* money off it for being such a big man. But I do it, and I'm a whore. Bullshit. I call fucking bullshit."

I wait several beats for him to reply. Creighton is gathering his words, and maybe his patience.

His voice is quiet when he finally speaks. "I'm sorry. I'm pissed. I've been saving up this fucking tirade for hours because you wouldn't answer your phone, and I shouldn't talk to you like that."

I hold the phone out and stare at it. *Is that really my brother? Apologizing?* Holly's had more of an effect on him than I realized. My defensiveness slips a few notches.

"I know; I shouldn't have done it. I didn't think about all the repercussions. I was hammered. Wasn't thinking clearly."

"I figured that one out. And now we're in a shitstorm that I'll get sorted out, but I need you to promise me this was a one-off and you're not following up with something bigger and better."

"Like a trip to Vegas and a wedding? No. My follow-up was handing in my resignation, and Ed is taking me home to become a hermit for the rest of my life."

"Resignation?" Creighton's shock comes through the phone line loud and clear. "Did they ask for it?"

I shake my head and then realize he can't see me. "No. In fact, they made it very clear that the firm didn't support my choice and I should make sure you understand that."

"Fuckers. I'll find a new firm anyway, especially if they made you feel like shit about it."

I almost don't say the words burning on my tongue, but I can't hold them in. "Like you just did?"

"I'm sorry, Greer. You deserve better than that."

"You're forgiven. I'll stay out of trouble, and you won't have to worry about my actions killing your stock price, okay?"

"You need me to come home? Circle the wagons? Kill anyone who looks at you the wrong way?"

That would be a whole lot of dead bodies, if my experience at the office is anything to go by. But I don't need my big brother to save me.

"It's okay. You need to be with Holly. Don't worry about me. I'll be fine."

"All right, but fucking answer the phone when I call so I don't lose my mind, okay?"

"Okay."

"Love you, Greer."

"Love you, Crey."

I hang up the phone and hand it back to Ed, meeting his eyes in the rearview mirror. "Thanks a lot."

"I was getting sick of answering his calls. He's just worried about you, Ms. Karas."

"I know."

I slouch back into the leather seat, thinking about what Creighton said as the familiar noises of Manhattan surround me all the way home.

CHAPTER FIVE

Cav

The cushy tan leather recliners in the private jet I get to use as part of my FleetJet subscription are a hell of a lot different from the tiny seat I was crushed into in coach the day I flew to LA with all my shit in two duffel bags. I avoided New York for three years by only doing interviews on the West Coast, but now I'm riding back in style.

The kind of style Greer Karas is accustomed to. I wonder absently if she has ever flown coach. Probably not.

The last time I saw her, there was no way I could give her that kind of life. It's funny how things change. But then again, some things never do. Like Greer and her *balls to the wall* style.

I chuckle as I tip back my Crown and Coke, remembering the first time we ever spoke . . .

The thick soles of my work boots sounded too loud on the marble floor, even with the nonstop chatter of the student coffee shop. These kids weren't all that much younger than me, but damn if they didn't make me feel old.

Of course, I saw her before I got in line. Greer Karas, sister to the infamous billionaire. But that wasn't why I couldn't keep my eyes off her. She was impossible to look away from. Beautiful in the kind of way that feels like a punch to the gut and a kick to the balls at the same time.

I placed my order. Black coffee. None of that frou-frou latte shit the law-school punks drank. As soon as I had the cup in hand, my eyes went back to her. Thick dark hair, sparkling dark eyes, smooth olive skin, knockout body with a curvy ass and perfect tits. Pure class stamped all over her.

She was also completely fucking oblivious nine-ty-nine percent of the time. The guys who stared at her ass went unnoticed, and so did the other chicks who sent her killing glares when their men couldn't help but follow the sway of her hips as she walked by. Her laugh was louder than the other girls', like she just didn't give a fuck who heard it because there was nothing she was going to do to corral it. Great laugh.

For three days, I'd spent more than I should have on this fancy coffee. I should have gone to the hole in the wall across the street where the rest of the maintenance crew and janitors went, but I couldn't stay away. Three days un-til I became painfully aware of that one percent of the time

Greer wasn't totally oblivious.

I settled into a chair at a tiny table in the corner, pulling out the newspaper I used as a distraction. When I looked up, I'd lost sight of her.

But she hadn't lost sight of me. Out of nowhere, she dropped into the chair across from me and spoke.

"You going to perv on me for a few more days before you finally drum up the courage to talk to me?"

Shocked, I sucked my coffee down the wrong pipe and hacked into my hand. My eyes watered as I took in her challenging and still curious grin. It wasn't a combination I'd seen before, but on her, it came off sexier than it should have.

"Excuse me?" I said when I could breathe again.

"You've been watching me. I've been waiting for you to invite me to sit down and have coffee with you, but you haven't. I gave you three days, and I'm sick of waiting." She set her coffee cup down on the table between us. "So I decided to take the initiative and brought my own."

Is this chick for real?

"I'm Greer."

I lowered my cup to the table. "You ever heard of letting the guy make the first move?"

She shrugged, and her tits pressed against her shirt in a way that made me want to take her into the maintenance closet and strip her naked. It wasn't the first time I'd had that thought. Or a whole fuck-ton of other thoughts about her. If she ever knew how bad I was twisted up over her . . .

Greer tucked her hair behind her ear and leaned forward on both elbows. "I told you, I gave you your chance.

You waited too long. Patience isn't one of my virtues."

I could imagine what some of her virtues were. Seizing an impulse, I held out my hand.

"I'm Cav."

Without hesitation, she shook it. Her hand felt so small in mine, but not fragile. No, based on that handshake, I knew she'd be able to hold her own with the asshole lawyers who'd be her coworkers in the not-too-distant future.

She released my grip and one dark eyebrow flew upward. *Shit, she's sexy.*

"That's it? Just Cav?"

"Ain't that enough for you?" I kept my tone cocky on purpose.

Her smile was quick and brilliant, the kind I felt below the belt. She turned my question around on me. "Is anything ever enough for a guy like you?"

She was sassy, a spitfire, and I wanted more of her, even if a guy like me had no business anywhere near her. I couldn't stop myself.

"I have a feeling you'd be more than enough, baby girl."

Her laugh, one I'd overheard so many times lately, rang out between us. She put her whole body into it. Held nothing back. I had to wonder if she'd be like that when I got her under me.

When? Fuck, I was screwed.

And yet I couldn't stop the image of me picking her up and fucking her against the wall from invading my brain. These pussy law school guys—her kind—couldn't fuck her like a real man. My work uniform wasn't going to hide the bulge in my pants for long. I needed to think about something else. Anything else.

The smile still tugging at the corners of her mouth when the laughter quieted wasn't helping the situation.

"How many girls have you used that line on, smooth talker?"

I lifted my coffee to my mouth and took a drink, managing not to choke this time. "I don't need lines. Hell, I don't even need to make an offer."

She followed my lead and raised her cup as well. The move made me wonder how easily she'd follow my lead in other areas.

"You're cocky as hell, but for some reason, I actually like it. But I don't dive right into bed with a guy. I deserve to be wooed first."

This time I did choke on my coffee again. "Wooed?"

Greer nodded. "Yeah, that's just the kind of girl I am, and lucky you—I'm giving you a shot at it."

Greer was every bit as cocky as me, even if she didn't realize it. I wasn't prepared to woo her then. But I am now.

That ad she posted wasn't as out of character for Greer Karas as the shocked world might imagine. It might have been a little bolder than her plopping down at my table in the coffee shop that day, but it was still the ballsy Greer I remembered.

I glance out the window at the flyover states below. A couple more hours, and I'll have the chance to reintroduce myself.

CHAPTER SIX

Greer

N o. *Fucking. Way.*

Can you photoshop real life? Because that's the only way I can possibly be seeing through my peephole what I'm seeing right now.

Cavanaugh Westman. In the flesh. Outside my door.

The knock stopped me mid-shuffle on the way to my coffeemaker. So that makes me an uncaffeinated, make-up-less, messy-bunned, legging-wearing couch surfer who hasn't showered in the two days I've spent holed up in my apartment.

He can't see me like this.

I've had so many fantasies of how it will go when I finally came face-to-face with Cav again. I'll be wearing something sexy, yet classy. Perfect hair, makeup, eyebrows. I'll adopt a casually disinterested mien. He'll be devastated when he realizes what he missed out on by standing me up that night and disappearing without a word.

There's no way in hell I'm answering that door. Cav Westman can sit out in my hallway all day. Not opening it.

But Cav reads my mind, the bastard.

"Open the door, baby girl. Your message came through loud and clear with that ad."

A barely audible gasp escapes my lungs.

"That's right, I know you're standing there. So, open the door, Greer."

His deep, gravelly voice stirs memories I thought I wiped out of my brain. *Apparently not.*

I rush to the couch to grab my phone. I need to text Banner. Need to freak out with her and schedule an emergency spa day so I can be all the things I need to be before facing him again.

My thoughts come to a screeching halt. *I do not need to impress Cav Westman. He's nothing to me. And I can prove it right now by opening the door. He'll see exactly how much I don't care about his opinion.*

Before I can change my mind, or look down at my shirt to make sure I'm not sporting any stains from yesterday's coffee, I reach for the dead bolts and unlock them before I twist the doorknob and tug.

As soon as the door is open, I know I've made a terrible mistake.

Through the peephole, he was marginally distorted. On the billboards and movie posters plastered to the sides of buses in the city, he looked like a total stranger. But Cav in the flesh?

Devastating.

I lose my grip on the door and it swings open.

How does he not look older? No new lines bracket his mouth or crease the corners of his eyes. Instead, a new scar curves along his jaw, giving him a sexier, more dangerous look. His shoulders are impossibly broader, making his hips seem even narrower.

His hazel eyes flash as he takes me in—at least they haven't changed. Today they're more tawny gold than gray or green. Guessing what color they would be was part of the game I played with myself before. His dark brown hair is sexy and disheveled, longer than the buzz cut he had before, but everything else is the same. Worn jeans, a plain T-shirt, and scuffed boots. Strong, bold features that many a man would find impossible to carry off, but are the reason millions of women would line up to have Cavanaugh Westman's babies.

"What are you doing here?" I whisper, reminding myself that I no longer have some naive fantasy of being *the one* for Cav.

His gaze returns to my face, and I know his inspection of me can't be nearly as flattering as mine of him.

I'm waiting for him to say something . . . anything. Like an apology or an explanation for disappearing three years ago, but instead I get something completely different.

His hands drop to the button of his jeans. "Based on your ad, the inspection isn't quite complete."

If my jaw could drop to the floor like a cartoon character's, it would.

Oh. My. God. I never saw what he was packing before, only a grazing handful the one night I finally got bold, but he put me off, promising me a night that never happened.

I stand like a slack-jawed moron and force my gaze to his face.

"What are you doing?"

His wicked grin—one he uses so rarely, even in the movies of his I'll never admit I've seen—wipes away the three years between our past and present.

The hiss of the zipper comes next.

I keep my gaze on his face as his eyes dare me. To look or to stop him, I'm not sure which.

"Apparently you've changed your requirements for wooing, baby girl."

The endearment on his lips brings back another wave of memories, but the flex of his bicep against the sleeve of his T-shirt steals my attention.

Oh. My. God.

He's gripping his cock, stroking it, isn't he? All I have to do is look down, and I'll have more than one question answered.

"You know you wanna look."

The dare is there again. And he's right. I want to look. So I do.

Sweet Jesus.

Oh. My. Hell.

Well, let's just say Cav knocked that requirement out of the park. The sight of his long, thick cock in his big, capable hand sends heat rushing south through my body, pooling between my thighs. My nipples, sans bra, strain against the material of my shirt. Cav's gaze drops as well—to my chest.

The room pulses with a desperate intensity. Hanging between us is the night we never had. The one he walked away from.

I have two choices. Take what I want, what I asked for, or hold on to the rejection he dealt me three years ago.

My brain short-circuits on one thought—life is short, and you never know if you'll get a second chance.

So I step forward, wrap one hand around his neck and the other around his cock, and kiss him for everything I'm worth.

CHAPTER
SEVEN

Cav

I groan into Greer's mouth as she grips my cock just above my hand. Taking charge of the kiss, I cup her jaw with my free hand and tilt her head for better access.

Perfect.

God, she's never looked more beautiful than she did the moment she opened the door. Totally and completely Greer. Real, not like the fake women I constantly meet in Hollywood. None of them compare to her. It ain't like you can compare a Chevy to a Ferrari.

And speaking of sweet curves . . . I release my hold on my dick and run my free hand up her side.

Mine. The taste of Greer on my lips and her body in my hands unleashes a wave of primal possessiveness. She's not the girl who got away; she's the one I walked away from. Life doesn't always give us second chances, but this one is mine and I'm taking it. And her.

I groan into her mouth again. The heat and lash of her tongue drag the sound from me. *Fuck*. I need more. Now.

Apparently I'm not the only one.

"My bedroom. Now."

Greer's voice is husky, and my cock is still wrapped by her hand as she jacks it. God, I've been dreaming about this moment for years.

"Fuck the bedroom. We're doing this right here."

I reach for her shirt and yank it over her head. She loses her grip on my cock for only a second, but it's long enough for me to toss the shirt and get my hands on her tits. She moans as I cup them.

"Goddamn, Greer. You were made for my hands."

I roll her nipples between my thumbs and fingers, and she arches toward me. Once she's moaning into my mouth, I release both handfuls and reach for the waistband of her pants, tugging them off just as quickly. Thank God for easy-to-remove clothing. One lift and I've got her ass in my hands as I turn toward the wall and press her back against it, exactly like I dreamed of doing that day in the coffee shop.

"Wrap your legs around my waist, baby."

She follows my direction, and I slide one hand between her legs.

Fuuck. She's soaked. Dripping for me.

Three years ago, I told myself I'd never feel the tight, sweet heat of her pussy. Three years ago, I told myself a lot of bullshit. Today, everything changes.

"Hurry," Greer whispers, her eyes closed as she rubs her pussy on my rock-hard cock. "I need it."

"Open your eyes, Greer," I say as I lift her and nudge the head against her opening.

She reaches down and helps guide my dick into place.

"Hurry," she says again.

"Look at me." In my commanding tone, it can't be interpreted as anything but an order.

Her dark eyes snap to mine, and I thrust.

Fucking. Perfection.

Holding her pinned to the wall, I fuck her like a man possessed, like a man with something to prove. And I do have something to prove. I'm fucking that piece-of-shit ex right out of her memory and burning myself in his place.

I can tell when I hit her sweet spot because Greer's nails dig into my shoulders and her keening moan fills my ears.

"Yes. Yes. Yes."

Never slowing my pace, I pound into her body as she grips me tighter and tighter, and finally yells my name as she comes.

The sound of my name on her lips unleashes my own orgasm. It pours out of me . . . directly into her.

Fuck. No condom. What the hell was I thinking? Oh, that's right. I wasn't thinking about anything but getting inside Greer after all these years.

With any other woman, I would worry about the possibility of her trying to trap me for my money or my fame. But not Greer. Fuck, but that doesn't mean I wouldn't try to trap her with a baby if that meant I could keep her.

I would lie, cheat, and steal to call this woman my own.

CHAPTER EIGHT

Greer

Oh. My. God. What the hell did I just do?

"Look at me."

Cav's gravelly voice breaks through the chaos crashing through my head and drowning out the amazing orgasm I just had. His order is the same as the one he gave before he slid that perfect cock inside me, and yet I can't look him in the eye this time.

I push against his shoulders. "I need to get down."

His grip tightens, and it's clear I'm going nowhere until he decides to let me off this ride.

"Greer, fucking look at me."

When I don't respond or comply, Cav's hand cups the side of my face and tilts it so I have no choice but to follow his order.

"Let me down."

"No."

A maniacal laugh breaks free from my lips. "You don't get to tell me no. Let me down now, dammit."

He shakes his head, and if I weren't so worried about holding on, I'd slap the smug look off his face.

"Finally got you where I want you, and I'm not letting you down until I'm ready."

"Where you want me? On your dick? You could've had me there three years ago, but we both know how that ended."

I shift again, my inner muscles reflexively clenching when his cock presses against me. *Isn't he going to get soft?*

Cav tightens his grip on my face. "There's a lot of shit you don't know, Greer."

My eyes roll so violently, I'm shocked I don't strain something. "Of course I don't know, because you didn't stick around long enough to say good-bye, let alone explain it to me."

The muscle in his jaw ticks, and I wish he'd set me down so I don't keep cataloging every shift in his expression. I'm under fire from Cav overload, and there's nowhere for me to go while he has me pinned on his cock. I'm truly between a cock and a hard place. Banner will never let me live this down.

I wait for an answer because I really have no choice in the matter. But the one I get from him isn't acceptable.

"I made the choice I had to make."

"And this is the choice I'm making—let me off your dick or I'm going to start screaming, and my neighbors are going to get a show they'll never forget." I make sure to enunciate every word.

His eyes flash, now golden brown with shafts of green. "I think you forgot. Putting on a good show is my job these days."

Anger seethes through me, and Cav must realize I'm about to lose my shit. He releases his hold on my face and wraps both hands around my waist to lift me off his cock, which is still crazy impressive. My feet hit the floor just as I realize we didn't use a condom.

How could I forget? I'm not an idiot kid. I'm a responsible, albeit unemployed, professional woman.

"Christ on a cracker. Isn't this rule number one in *fucking as a Hollywood star*? Wrap it up? What if you knocked me up? Aren't you afraid I'll smear you in the tabloids? 'Cav Westman's Baby Mama Love Child Scandal.'" I gesture with my hand as I turn away and stalk toward my bathroom to clean up.

I freeze when I set foot in front of the mirror. *Hot. Mess.* My hair is wild, clearly from the *just been fucked* school of hair styling. The look in my eyes is even wilder than my hair.

Shower. That's my only option right now. I turn the water to scalding and step right into the stream.

What the hell did I just do?

Cav Westman shows up out of nowhere because my crazy ad actually caught his attention, and then he whips his dick out, I grab it, and he bangs me against a wall.

I grab a bottle of body wash and squeeze a quarter of the bottle into my hand, as though the suds can somehow wash away the domino effect of bad judgment invading my life recently.

What a freaking disaster.

I'm reaching for the shampoo, still giving myself a mental scolding, when I feel a rush of cold air behind me.

"Careful, baby girl. You're gonna scrub yourself raw if you don't take it easy."

Water washes the bubbles from my body and I spin around to face him.

He's naked. Droplets splash off me and bead on his skin, sliding down one tanned inch at a time, rolling over muscles and sinew.

Words escape me as I watch one specific drop roll toward his cock. Why does he have to be so damn beautiful? He shouldn't be allowed to be naked near me. I won't be able to stop myself from touching him.

Then stop looking at him, Greer.

For the purpose of self-preservation only, I turn and face the wall and attempt to act casual. Like I'm going to be able to continue my regular shower routine while Cav Westman's perfect naked body stands only feet away from me.

I grab my shampoo and squirt way too much into my hand because I'm concentrating really hard on the white grout between my cream-and-gold-flecked travertine tiles and not the naked man behind me.

"What are you doing in here?" I'm going for nonchalant, but the words come out strained.

"Following you."

"Without an invitation?"

His husky laugh fills the shower enclosure. "The sight

of your gorgeous ass walking away was the only invitation I needed."

I turn again, this time determined to keep my eyes on his face. Except his eyes are *not* on mine. Nope, he's taking in every inch of my nakedness, and my skin heats from more than the scalding water.

He steps closer, murmuring something that's lost in the pounding of the spray.

"What did you say?"

The golden brown of his irises seems to glow. "Wasted three years. Not going to waste any more time."

My heart slams against my chest. I can't handle declarations like that from him. All my life, I've had an overarching sense of loss that started with never knowing my parents. That loss was exacerbated by having a brother who was sent away to boarding school when I was young. An uncle who was cold and distant and now missing. An aunt who alternately doted on me or pretended I didn't exist, depending on my uncle's mood. And then the time I started to fall for the guy standing before me and thought I might have found something real, but then he disappeared without a word.

No one stays in my life. At least, not for long.

With each slow breath I take, I reel in my rioting emotions, forcing my heart to slow to a regular pace. When I posted that ad, I was drunk and looking for validation. Someone to make Tristan realize he missed out on the awesomeness that is me. I couldn't even truly admit to myself that I held a sliver of hope that this particular man would see it. I never expected it to work, and I certainly wasn't prepared for the tidal wave of emotions that would come with it when it did.

I need space, but Cav clearly has other ideas because he's moving closer. *I can't do this.* If Cav's water-slicked body presses mine against the wall and his lips find all the spots that make me shiver and moan . . . it will push me down a path I'm not sure I'm ready for.

What the hell was I thinking when I placed that ad? I wasn't thinking. That's the problem. But I'm thinking now.

"I . . . I think you should go." My voice wavers on the first words, but strengthens as I find my conviction.

Cav doesn't listen. Instead he steps closer, crowding me into the tiled corner. "Are you sure that's what you really want, baby girl? Because I think you'd rather I pin you to this wall and fill that perfect little pussy over and over until your screams bounce off these walls. I think you want me to help you forget that piece-of-shit loser who came before me. I can wipe him away, Greer. You'll never remember any cock but mine. Never remember any orgasm as good as the ones I'm about to give you."

The vision of what he described comes to life in my mind, and dammit, I want that. I want him. I want to forget the frenzied thoughts warring in my head. Maybe, just maybe, for once in my life I can stop thinking and go with what feels right.

Except the last time you did that with him, you got burned.

Sitting alone on the Top of the Rock, waiting for Cav to show. And he never did. The hair, makeup, and everything else I spent an entire day preparing for that one night

. . . for nothing. And I never heard a word from him again.

He walked away then, which means he can easily walk away now.

I shake my head. "Go. Please. This was a huge mistake." The words grate against my throat, sounding as forced as they truly are.

I keep my eyes lowered to the side, counting the tiles on my shower wall rather than meeting his gaze. When he doesn't move, I squeeze them shut and wait.

Another cold rush of air signals his exit. Because that's what Cav is good at—leaving.

I stay in the bathroom for much longer than I need to, killing time because I don't want to face what I've done. Five minutes, that's about how long it took for me to let a guy I hadn't seen in years fuck me. No explanation. No discussion. Just sex.

I would call myself a slut, but I don't believe in double standards.

And then there's the small matter of the fact that we didn't use a condom. I will call myself an idiot because that's the absolute truth. I'm on the pill, but I don't know where Cav has *been*. If there's any truth to the tabloids, I just fucked half of Hollywood. *Ick.*

Right, so doctor's appointment next. And then I'm going to get to work on the case I snatched out of my office. I've spent two days in a woe-is-me pity party, and it's time to get my ass in gear.

Feeling better about my decisions, I blow-dry my hair and apply my makeup. Finally looking less like a homeless waif who found her way into my apartment, I enter my bedroom through the connecting door to find clothes. Part of me wonders if I'll find Cav sprawled out there, waiting for round two, but that would be a no. Grabbing a clean pair of leggings, a bra, and a T-shirt, I quickly toss them on.

I'm stepping out of my bedroom when I hear the sounds coming from the kitchen.

No. Way.

That's my first thought when I see Cav sliding an omelet onto one of my plates.

"Hash browns are almost done. Hope you're hungry."

I must have stepped into an alternate universe. Because that's the only explanation I have for the fact that Cav is cooking breakfast in my kitchen.

"What are you doing?" I ask, my question ridiculously obvious and dumb.

"I'm hungry. Didn't take the time to grab any food before I came."

Okay, time for an awkward reality check.

I drop a hand to my hip and lift my chin. "Speaking of coming, do you have anything I need to be worried about? I mean, I'll still get checked and I'm on the pill, but it'd be good to know what I'm walking into."

Cav shakes his head as he lifts the hash browns out of the pan and onto the plates. "I would think you'd know better than to believe every damn thing you read in the tabloids, Greer. I might be a dick, but I'm not a total manwhore. You hungry?" He finally looks at me when he holds out the plate.

I don't know what to say as I take the plate from him besides, "Thank you."

Yes, definitely alternate reality. I'm sitting at the bar in my kitchen with Cavanaugh Westman beside me, and we're eating omelets and hash browns. How the hell did this happen?

And of course, the ridiculous girl inside me says, *This isn't exactly a story we can tell our grandchildren about how we reunited.*

We are not having grandchildren, Greer! We're having no children. We're not even a we.

I keep sneaking sideways glances at Cav as we eat. His jawline is covered in just enough scruff to make me wonder what it would feel like against my thighs.

Abort, Greer. Abort. I've got to stop thinking that way about him.

Memories from the first time I spotted him filter through my brain . . .

Who is that guy? His navy blue work pants fit his thick thighs and tight ass to perfection. Every other man I'd ever seen in those kind of pants—the ones with the bar code patch on the waistband for the cleaning company to scan that peeked out from beneath a heavy canvas belt—had a flat man-ass or a plumber's crack that no one ever wanted to see.

But not this guy. The blue-gray work shirt made his eyes appear steel gray. The sleeves were rolled up over thick, corded forearms, revealing words inked along his golden-brown skin.

I glanced around to see if anyone else in the café noticed my detailed survey of the hottest maintenance man on the planet, but all I could see was the other girls' eyes glued to him. Nope, I wasn't the only person to notice him.

His dark hair was buzzed short and a sexy five o'clock shadow shaded his jaw, even though it was only noon. His broad shoulders and narrow waist probably had us all thinking the same thing—if there was a God in heaven, this man was actually a stripper and not the maintenance man, and we were about to get the greatest show of our lives when he tore that shirt off. From beneath the unbuttoned collar, I caught a glimpse of a white wife beater. Add in the tool bag he carried and my fantasies were spinning wildly out of control.

"Dibs," Tracey whispered to me as we flipped through our flash cards for our Secured Transactions class.

I was supposed to know what a purchase-money security interest was, but all I could think about was the guy ordering something from the barista a dozen feet away from me. Black coffee, that was my guess. He didn't look the type to order anything so feminine as a latte or a cappuccino. Nor did he seem like the double espresso type.

"What did you say?" My attention shifted reluctantly from what he was ordering to my friend.

Tracey tossed her flash cards on the table. "Never mind. I rescind my dibs. Honestly, I wouldn't know what to do with that much man, even in my dreams."

I grab the flash card on the top of the pile, forcing my brain back into study mode. "Purchase-money security interest. That's what we need to be talking about. Professor Payne is going to call on me. I feel it."

Tracey groaned. "It's not your day; it'll be mine. I feel it. Fuck the Socratic method so hard."

She grabbed the rest of the cards and read off the elements of a purchase-money security interest. I completely tuned her out as the guy came toward us and his gaze collided with mine.

Holy hell. I felt it rake over my skin and take in every detail of my appearance. I was wearing skinny jeans, tall boots, and a sweater. My hair was falling down around my shoulders, and I was on the verge of pulling it back into a messy bun. I was glad I hadn't yet, though.

Why did I even care? He was no one to me. But I wanted him to be.

"Greer, did you get that?"

"Huh?"

Tracey tossed the flash cards down again and wrapped her hands around her coffee cup. She watched me as she brought it to her lips. "You're totally eye-fucking that guy and not using a single brain cell for Secured Trans."

I jerked my gaze away from his and back to Tracey. "Uh, I don't know what you're talking about. I'm just . . . you know. What?"

The incoherent babbling gave me away. Or my complete and utter lack of subtlety. But dammit, the guy was hot and nothing like the Polo-shirt-wearing boys I went to school with. Their arms and shoulders did not look like that. Who knew a work uniform could be so dang sexy? And there I went again.

"Sorry. Secured Trans. Purchase-money security interest requires . . ." and I rattled off the elements.

Tracey's eyes widened. "I hate that you're so smart sometimes. You haven't been paying attention at all, and you still know exactly what you need to know. Finish your eye-fucking and let's get to class."

"Greer," Cav says, and from his tone, it sounds like it isn't the first time he said my name.

I shake my head and drag myself into the present, to the man sitting beside me who has haunted my thoughts for years.

"What'd you say?"

"Something wrong with the food? You on a hunger strike?"

I look down at my plate. I've only taken one bite, and the rest of the omelet is untouched.

"No. No, it's fine. I'm just . . . processing what the hell is going on here. I didn't exactly expect . . ."

"Me to show up at your door?"

I sneak another sideways glance and take in his raised eyebrow and the huge bite he shovels into his mouth. His omelet is three times the size of mine and almost gone. How the man can eat that much and still be so ripped is beyond me.

"Yeah." I dig my fork into my own food, even though my stomach is a jumble of nerves right now and I don't actually know how much I can eat.

"Well, what the fuck did you expect me to do when I saw the posts about the ad? You weren't exactly subtle."

I chew my light, fluffy eggs and bacon—*mmm, bacon*—as I consider my answer. I choose the truth. "I didn't expect you to remember me. You're a Hollywood big shot, and I'm the girl you stood up years ago."

Okay, so it's not the complete truth because some tiny absurd part of me insists he couldn't forget me when I could never forget him.

Cav's fork clatters against his plate as he turns. He slips the utensil from my hand and sets it on the counter.

"Do you really fucking think that?" His eyes flash golden-green and his brows draw together. This is the *Cav is pissed* look.

"What? That you walked away and never looked back? It certainly seems accurate. Unless you want to tell me you were thinking of me the whole time you were fucking Windsor Reed too?"

The gossip sites were overrun with news of the two of them for the last year. And yes, I read all the articles, despite telling myself I wouldn't every single time.

"I never stopped thinking about you. I sure as hell didn't walk away and never look back. I've never forgotten a single thing."

"Then why did you do it?"

"I didn't have a choice." His jaw muscle ticks, and I know there's a lot more to the story than what he's telling me.

"You always have a choice." That's one thing I believe without question.

"I didn't then, but I do now. And I'm here." His eyes plead that he's sincere, and yet I still can't trust him.

"No other explanation? What would you do if you were me, Cav? What if I'd been the one to stand you up and bail out of your life for three years with no word? Wouldn't you have questions? Want a few more answers that weren't total bullshit?"

He doesn't even blink. If anything, his stare gets more intent. I'm unable to look away, hostage to his gaze.

"I'd thank whatever gods and devils I needed to that you found your way back into my life, and I'd worry about the details later. You wanted this, Greer. You never would've posted that ad if you didn't. So, what's it gonna take to make it right? You want me to grovel? Because I'm not the kind of man who will ever do that. But if you want proof that I'm here for real, I won't stop until you believe it."

I look away first. Cav has always been so damn intense—a force unto himself. Whatever his reasons were for leaving, it's clear I'm not getting the explanation I want so desperately.

Can I live with that? I don't know.

He climbs off the bar stool and grabs his plate, then tosses the rest of the omelet in the trash. I watch wordlessly as he rinses the plate, lays it in the sink, wipes his hands, and heads for the door.

"Make up your mind, Greer. This time it's not a game."

CHAPTER
NINE

Greer

Cav's words play in a loop in my head as I gear up to interview my client. I've never been to Rikers Island before, and if Creighton knew I was going, he'd put me under 24/7 security. When my driver gives me a double take at the address I deliver, I know it's only a matter of time before my brother finds out.

My tattletale of a driver texts him immediately, and my phone rings.

"Please tell me you did not just ask to be driven to Rikers Island, Greer."

Glaring at Ed, I mouth, *Really?*

"Hello, darling brother, how are you? I'm fine. Just salvaging some self-worth by continuing to work after I quit my job that I should've been fired from but they were afraid of you."

"Greer . . ." Creighton's growl carries over the line, and I can hear roadies in the background and someone calling out orders.

I really don't want to get into the same conversation we had last time, so I jump on a subject guaranteed to grab his attention. "How's Holly? The baby bump is looking so damn cute in the pictures I've been seeing online."

"Don't even try to change the subject."

Plan? Fail.

"Seriously, Crey. I'm working. It's not a big deal. Their security is tight, and I'm in absolutely no danger. Stand. Down."

"If I were in the city right now, I'd go with you myself. You need to take Ed inside with you. I'm not taking chances with your safety. Who the hell are you interviewing anyway? And we have a whole shitload of other stuff to discuss. Like why you've suddenly decided prisoners' rights is an appropriate use of your free time."

"I'll make sure Ed comes inside with me. I won't go alone. I'm not an idiot."

With that, Ed puts the car into drive and we're officially headed to Rikers. God, I hope this isn't just one more bad decision in a long line of bad decisions I've made lately.

"You know I'm worried about you."

"I know, but you should worry about your wife and your baby on the way."

My subject change works like a champ this time.

"Holly's fine. Radiant, actually. I'm going to keep her barefoot and pregnant for as long as I can."

I laugh, and it's the first genuine humor I've felt in days. "You better watch yourself. If she overhears you, she's going to tear you a new one." My sister-in-law is nothing if not feisty.

"I'm already getting the look of death from across the room, but thank you for your concern."

"Where are you?"

"Denver, tonight anyway. Who the hell knows tomorrow. We'll be back in Nashville next week, and she's done with touring until after the baby is born."

A giant grin stretches across my face. I'm going to be an auntie, and I can't wait to spoil my new niece rotten.

"That sounds like a good plan. Keep her happy, Crey. I'll talk to you soon."

Creighton starts to say something else, but I'm sure it's just going to be more orders, so I hang up. When my phone doesn't start ringing again immediately, I count myself lucky. Being Creighton Karas's little sister isn't the easiest thing in the world, but I wouldn't trade it for anything.

The drive out to Rikers is long enough to set my nerves on edge, especially as we approach the prison. There's a really good reason I didn't go into criminal defense, namely, the criminals. So, why did I grab the damn file? I could have left it and never worried about it again. The firm would have had me withdrawn from the case, and I could have tried out *carefree trust-fund princess* as a job title. But apparently that's not something I'm capable of.

I'm cursing my decision as we work our way through security, and then again as I wait alone in the interview area. Creighton's going to be pissed if he learns the guards won't let Ed inside the room for the interview because he doesn't have proper clearance in advance. Let's hope Ed decides to leave that fact out of his report to Creighton. A guard stands not more than six feet away, so I take comfort in that.

But when Stephen Cardelli steps into the interview room in shackles, my heart rate picks up. *I can do this. I can do this. I'm on his side. He's not going to hurt me.*

There's something about his self-satisfied smile that instantly makes me feel dirty. Swallowing back the fear, I stand and nod.

"Mr. Cardelli. Thank you for agreeing to sit down with me to discuss your case. I apologize for not getting here sooner."

"If I'd known you were such a sweet young thing, I'd have been a hell of a lot more interested in talking to my lawyer."

Deep breaths. *Be professional, Greer.* I flip open my file and read through issues enumerated in his complaint.

"Can you tell me, in your own words, more about the issues you're claiming impinge on your constitutional rights?"

He smiles again, his teeth yellow and brown near the edges, and his greasy gray hair falling over his forehead. "Let's talk about the fact that I didn't commit the murder they say I did. I was framed. And you're going to get me out of here."

Uh, nope. I certainly would not be doing that.

"I'm sorry, Mr. Cardelli, this is not an Innocence Project case. You filed a prisoners' rights complaint and that's what I'm here about. If you think you've been wrongfully convicted, I can give you information about the Innocence Project and they may be able to help you. In the meantime, perhaps we can help you win this case and make your life a little more palatable inside these walls."

His smile morphs into an angry glare that's fierce enough to scare the living hell out of me. "If you think there's jack shit you can do to make life inside *palatable*, then you're dead fucking wrong, girl. You want to hear the real story?"

"Sir, I understand you must be very frustrated, but I'm limited to the case before me."

"Well, listen the fuck up, bitch. You're gonna do what I tell you." He stands and the guard is by his side within seconds, hands on his shoulders, slamming him back into the chair.

"Sit the fuck down, Cardelli, or this interview is over."

Cardelli bares his teeth like an animal, and I'm doubly glad this case has nothing to do with getting him out of here.

"Fine. Get the guards to stop shoving their batons up my fucking ass, and maybe it'll be a little more fucking palatable."

"Done, Cardelli. You're fucking done." The guard yanks him out of his seat and drags him toward the door.

I'm pretty sure the guard shouldn't be allowed to do that because this is a meeting with counsel, but at the moment, I'm not moved to protest. I'm in over my head and I know it.

Work through the fear, Greer. Pull up your big-girl panties and step outside your little bubble of a world to do something for someone who doesn't have anyone else fighting for him.

Why couldn't I have some kind of battered-woman case? Someone I feel sympathy for? Someone who doesn't scare the shit out of me?

Maybe this is some sort of a test. Maybe this is exactly what I need. Penance for the stupid stunt I pulled that cost me my job in the ivory tower.

When the guard returns, my hands are still shaking as I shove papers back into my file.

"Sorry about that, Ms. Karas. He's not a good one. You might want to hand this case off to someone else. Don't think this is right for you."

The guard's patronizing attitude pisses me off, and quite frankly, makes me all the more determined not to give it up.

"Thank you for your concern, but I'm a professional. I'm more than capable of handling this case."

"What would your brother say about that?"

Oh. No. He. Didn't.

I smile brightly, my face about to split wide open from the force of the fake expression. "I'm sure that's none of your business or his. Now, could you please show me out? My driver is waiting."

The guard leads me out of the interview room and through the maze of hallways and secured doors. I don't breathe easy until I reach the waiting area where Ed is sitting.

"Thank you for waiting."

He studies me, his attention pausing and holding on my shaking hands as they grip the file. "You okay, Ms. Karas? You look a little pale."

I dig out the fake smile again. "I'm fine. Let's head back to the city."

CHAPTER

TEN

Cav

I pound on Greer's door, and I don't fucking care that I left with the ball in her court, determined for the next move to be hers. This shit don't fly.

Greer tugs the door open, still dressed in dress pants and an expensive-looking blouse.

"What the fuck did you think you were doing?" I demand, pushing through the opening and slamming the door behind me.

"How did you get up here again? This is a secured building. They can't just let you up. You're not on my list."

"Baby girl, I'm on every fucking list these days. Now answer my goddamn question. What the fuck were you doing at Rikers?"

Her glare is cute, but not cute enough to distract me from the verbal ass whupping I'm about to lay on her.

"My job."

"You don't have a fucking job, Greer. You quit."

"How do you even know all this? You're worse than my brother. If you're keeping tabs on me, you need to stop. I'll tell you what I want you to know, when I want you to know it."

I step closer to her, gripping her chin with my hand. "That's not how this works, Greer. Not when you decide to put yourself into situations where you don't belong. Who the fuck were you meeting in Rikers?"

"None of your goddamn business. Now back off." She shoves at my chest, but I don't move.

"If your brother isn't going to keep a leash on you to keep you safe, then I will, because clearly you can't be trusted to make the right choices when it comes to your personal safety."

As soon as the words are out of my mouth, I know they're the wrong thing to say, but I don't care. There are few circumstances under which I'm willing to piss Greer off, and anything having to do with her safety is one of them. She can fight me all she wants. It's a pointless battle she won't win.

"I'm afraid that's confidential. As in attorney-client privilege, you asshole. Now back off." She shoves at my chest again.

"I leave you for a few hours and you run right to the nearest place you could get shanked. Smart, Greer. Really fucking smart."

She crosses her arms and stares me down. "It wasn't like I wandered down a dark alley in the Bowery in the middle of the night by myself. There were guards. Security. He was in shackles. I'm fine. And I am fucking smart, so don't be a dick or I'll call security right now and toss your ass out. Were you always this overbearing? Did I forget somehow?"

Only one word of her little speech penetrates my anger. "Shackles? Who the fuck were you meeting with? A murderer?"

Greer's little growl would be cute if my vision weren't turning red. She needs a keeper.

She doesn't have a quick, snarky reply, and that's when I realize I'm right.

"Fuck, Greer. This is done. Whatever case you're working on *while you're unemployed* is over."

"You don't get to give orders here. I'm not asking for your permission. You've been back in my life for less than twenty-four hours, and I'm already questioning why I wanted you back so badly."

That penetrates. I rein in my rage and calm the fuck down. But she still needs to understand that her safety isn't something to be taken lightly.

"You wanted me back so badly because you know I give a fuck, and I'm not a pussy like the last guy who clearly didn't have two brain cells to rub together if he fucked things up with you."

Her mouth drops open. "Oh, you're one to talk."

"Shut up, Greer. I'm here. I'm not leaving. And if you're not going to make your safety a priority, I will."

I think about adding something about her brother agreeing with me, but I have a hunch it would be less well-received than the rest of my decree. Either way, Greer needs to wise up and quick.

"I'm not dropping the case." Her tone is downright mulish.

"Then I'm going with you next time. Nonnegotiable."

Greer's brows draw together, confusion clear on her face. "How long are you staying in New York? Don't you have a movie to get back to somewhere?"

"I bought a place here. I'll be here as long as I can, and figure out something that works."

Her eyes widen with shock. "You bought a place? In New York? You haven't been back to the city in the entire time you've done the acting gig, and all of a sudden you're homesick enough to buy a place?"

"You gave me a reason," I say, keeping it simple.

"And I wasn't reason enough before?" Her question comes out quietly.

I drop my hold on her chin and grip the back of my neck. "It's not that simple. I had to make something of myself first. I couldn't come back until now."

Greer shakes her head. "I don't understand."

I stare into her beautiful dark eyes and give it to her straight. "Do you really think your brother would've let you date a maintenance guy, Greer? Would he ever believe I was after anything but your money? Do you think I'd ever be able to respect myself if he thought that?"

Realization dawned over her delicate features. "It never mattered to me. And what my brother thinks shouldn't have mattered to you either. Do you really believe I'm that shallow? That I gave a fuck what you did for a living?"

"It's called pride, Greer. I wasn't about to swallow it. I couldn't come to you until I was an equal. And when I finally got there, you were dating a guy who was from your world. What the fuck was I supposed to do? Come in and crash something I thought made you happy?"

"Is that the only reason you stayed away this long?" she asks.

I look her dead in the eye and lie. "Yes."

CHAPTER ELEVEN

Greer

"Oh my God, he fucked you up against the wall?" Banner's gushing over drinks the day after Cav and I had the Rikers discussion that ended in a stand-off. "This guy gets my vote for sure."

"Shhh . . ." I glance around to see if anyone else heard her from this isolated corner in the loud bar. No heads are swinging this way, so I consider it a lucky break. "He bought a condo in my building, B. He says he's staying for a while. Waiting on some contract to get worked out for his next role, so he's got time to kill in between."

She picks up her dirty martini and sips. "So, when do I get to meet him? This is the friend-approval stage, and we need to check all the boxes this time around."

Last time around, Tracey approved of Cav mightily, and even with a hint of jealousy. Sadness pangs me when

I think of her. Three months before graduation, and only days before Cav disappeared, she was killed in a hit-and-run near the law school.

Even now, it seems so senseless and inexplicable. Survivor's guilt still plagues me because I should have been with her—we were training for a couch to half marathon—and I would have been if Creighton hadn't asked me to accompany him to a meeting to sign a bunch of paperwork for my trust.

"I guess you'll get to meet him when I figure out what the hell I'm going to do with him."

Banner eyes me with confusion. "Do with him? We've already determined what you're going to do with him— let him bang you repeatedly up against walls. Bent over counters and couches work too. And in the shower. Wait until you get bored to start fucking in a bed. Oh, and elevators. Maybe the backseat of a limo?"

Her list of suggestions comes way too rapidly for her not to have spent some time thinking about this. But then again, she's Banner, so she's always thinking about this. She should have been a writer or something, but Banner always goes her own way.

"I haven't even decided if I'm going to . . . bang him again."

Her expression is comical. If her jaw could drop any further, it would be nearing the table. "Are you shitting me? Girl, you were born to walk a red carpet on the arm of a man that gorgeous. And I'm going to Hollywood to find one of my own, tagging along with your little party."

And it all becomes clear. "You're going to use me and

Cav to find yourself a man?"

"Hell yes! What best friend wouldn't? I'm sexy. I'm single. Some guy would be lucky as hell to lock down this ass. If I ever give one the chance."

She's right. Any guy would be lucky to have a shot with her, if she'd give them a chance past the first date. Banner is most definitely an *I fuck on the first date* kind of girl, because she doesn't usually go back for seconds and she's got "needs."

I guess she rubbed off on me because I didn't wait past the first five minutes to get naked with Cav. Or then again, I guess you could say I waited way too long for that. After I finally got up the nerve to talk to him the first time around, it was another few weeks of flirting before we moved to the next level. All leading up to the night he stood me up.

I know I can't take another step forward with Cav until I come to terms with what happened before. We have no future if I can't let it go. I won't be the bitter woman holding something over her man's head for the rest of his life; I'm not built like that. But I also have enough self-awareness to know that my abandonment issues aren't easily overcome.

"Earth to Greer. We've got incoming . . ."

I look to Banner and then in the direction she's tilting her head. Every person in the bar is chattering now with the arrival of Cavanaugh Westman. Good grief, does the guy not know how to go incognito? Shouldn't that be Hollywood 101, along with the condom thing? Then again, maybe he just makes his own rules.

It takes me a moment to realize he's not alone. There

are two large, burly guys following behind him. Security? *Wow. Not something I expected.*

Cav finds our table quickly, nodding as he passes through the crowd of gawkers. The two security people keep the crowd away as he slides into the booth beside me.

"What'd I miss, baby girl?"

"Huh-uh. Excuse me? What are you—"

He leans in and presses a kiss to my cheek, stalling out the rest of my stammered words.

"Stopped by your place to pick you up for dinner, but you were gone. Doorman was nice enough to let me know your regular haunts."

"Traitor. His Christmas bonus may be less impressive this year," I say under my breath.

"Hi! I'm Banner," my friend says brightly, holding out a hand. "I'm just letting you know that if you don't get the friend seal of approval, we're going to have issues. You want me to like you. It's pretty damn important."

Cav grips Banner's hand and shakes it. "It's nice to meet you. I'm glad Greer has you around to weed out the assholes."

Banner grins. "She doesn't always listen to me. Exhibit A, Tristan." She shakes her head, and I want to bean her with an olive.

A glance around reveals a crowd of onlookers and more than a few flashing cameras. I've seen enough with Creighton and Holly to know that what's happening right now is going to make the gossip rags. Cav doesn't seem to care at all, though, as he slides his arm around me, his other hand resting on my thigh. The gesture is one hundred percent possessive.

"Fair enough. If you've got a problem with me, lay it out. I'm not afraid to work for something that matters."

"From what I hear, you've already put in some serious work." Banner winks conspiratorially.

Yep, she deserves an olive right between her perfectly arched eyebrows.

"Really? Friendship foul, B."

She lifts her drink, salutes me, and sucks it down. I turn my attention back to the man beside me, or rather, surrounding me, as he doesn't seem to understand the concept of personal space.

I shift just enough to put an inch of space between our thighs. Cav immediately moves closer, his heat soaking into me.

"What are you doing here? And what's with the goons? You didn't even try one of your hip Hollywood disguises?"

Cav's arm tightens around my shoulders. "I've got no problem with the world knowing you're mine."

Then it dawns on me. He's staking a claim. A very public one.

"What's your angle? Is this you trying to save my reputation?"

He and I both know that my character is still being savaged in the media. Even with Creighton's PR team playing cleanup crew, there's no stopping it.

Cav fingers a lock of my hair. "I've never played a white knight role, but I'd like to think I could pull it off."

"Villains are even better," Banner quips. "Just sayin'. And the ad is kinda my fault. So feel free to save the distressed lady's reputation."

Cav grins as Banner makes her confession, and I have no explanation for why I'm so envious that she's on the receiving end of his smile. This man . . . he makes me crazy.

"Why am I not surprised that putting the two of you together with a hell of a lot of alcohol will end with bat-shit-crazy stuff every time?" He shakes his head, looking from me to Banner. "I owe you a big thank-you, Banner. You've got my marker. Anytime you need a favor, just let me know."

He has no idea what he's just done. Clearly. Because I can already see Banner's brain working overtime. She's going to be cashing in this favor for a Hollywood insider's trip.

Banner rubs her hands together with a mischievous smile. "I really hope you're ready to deliver when the time comes."

Cav just smiles confidently. "How about I buy you another round first?"

CHAPTER

TWELVE

Cav

Sitting here in the bar with Greer and her friend, I can't help but remember the first bar I ever went to with the woman sitting beside me who keeps trying to put space between us. What she doesn't realize is that her chance at putting any distance between us is gone. She blew that right out of the water the moment her hand wrapped around my cock for the first time.

Our second round arrives, and my memories surface as Greer and Banner banter back and forth across the table . . .

I knew it was a bad idea before we even walked in the door. I didn't belong in this bar with this woman on my arm. Sure, it was a student haunt and a hole-in-the-wall, but I was the only guy in this place without a collared shirt and an overinflated ego fueled by Mommy and Daddy's money.

And yet here I was, because apparently I would follow Greer anywhere, including to the empty corner booth. Her jeans hugged her rounded ass, and I wasn't the only one who noticed. I shot a look of death at one skinny little punk who was probably popping a half chub just watching her. When he finally realized he'd caught my attention, his gaze fell away.

That's right, kid. She's out of your league. Fuck, she was out of my league too, but I wasn't going to let that deter me.

I didn't care about the looks that Greer got. She deserved every single one of them, even if she was totally oblivious. But I wasn't oblivious. My possessive instincts climbed with every pair of eyes that fixed on her ass. They could look, but she was mine.

Except she wasn't really, and I was screwing with myself if I believed she could be.

I was the maintenance guy. She was a trust-fund princess.

The attention that followed her landed on me as I slid into the booth beside her. Shock. The *what the fuck is she doing with him* looks. I met the gaze of another little prick, daring him to make a move. He wouldn't. None of them would. They wouldn't even know how to get their hands dirty.

Including the princess across from me. But why wasn't

I holding that against her? *Because you want to be inside her*, my inner voice said. And it was right. I wasn't supposed to be fascinated by this girl, but it was impossible not to be. She was like a goddamned magnet and I couldn't stay away, even though I should.

A server came to the table. No surprise, it was a guy.

"Hey, Greer, want your usual?"

She smiled politely and nodded, but he didn't walk away or ask for my order.

"Have you started your outline yet for Corporations? I've got a study group, if you want in."

"I'll take a Bud, in a bottle," I said, interrupting his blatant pickup attempt that ignored the fact I was sitting beside her.

"I don't want to talk about school tonight," Greer said. "Catch you tomorrow or something?"

The server nodded sheepishly. "Sure. Sorry. I'll get those drinks right out." His attention finally landed on me, and just like the rest of them, I could see the question of why I was with her burning in his brain.

I sat up and put my arms on the table, shoving my shirtsleeves up my forearms and revealing the sleeve of ink stopping at my wrist. His eyes darted from my arms to my face. Little fuck was probably assuming it was prison ink.

Assume away, especially if it gets you out of our faces faster.

He turned away, mumbling something I couldn't make out.

I shifted my attention back to Greer. She was completely oblivious to the posturing that had just happened. Her wide eyes were glued on my tattoos, which weren't normally visible with my long-sleeved work shirt.

Did the princess have a problem with the maintenance guy being tatted up? Her words put an end to my wondering immediately, as did the fingertips that ran over the ink.

"Oh wow. I didn't know you had tattoos. I want one, but I'm not quite ready to make it happen."

Memories of that night play through my head as I listen to the two women. There's definitely a difference between then and now. Tonight, eyes are on me for a different reason—not because I don't belong with Greer, but because she and I are equally matched. I belong in her world in a way I never did before.

Now I just have to convince her of that.

One thing hasn't changed—Greer is still completely oblivious to the reasons for the looks she gets. She thinks it's because of the notoriety of the ad, but that's not it. At least, not completely. She's got no clue that she's the total package.

It blows my mind that her boyfriend would cheat. Definitely missing brain cells, but I owe him a thank-you. If not for that, she might never have placed the ad, and I wouldn't have gotten the signal loud and clear that my second chance had arrived.

"You're gonna take good care of my girl now, aren't you? Make sure she gets home?" Banner's words slur together as she climbs out of the car driven by Greer's driver, Ed.

"I've got it covered."

As Banner stumbles toward the door, I tell the driver, "Would you follow her up to her apartment and make sure she gets inside?"

Ed's already climbing out of the car. "Of course, sir."

Greer snuggles into me as the door shuts. "That was a good idea."

"Can't be too careful."

I watch through the large windows in the lobby as Banner grabs Ed's arm and allows him to lead her into the elevator as she waves to the doorman.

"How drunk are you, Greer?" I pull her onto my lap sideways and stare into her shining brown eyes.

"Drunk enough but not too drunk. I'm perfect." Her words aren't as slurred as Banner's, but she's beyond tipsy.

"Which means?"

"I'm drunk enough to want you to take me back to my apartment and do dirty things to me, but not too drunk to enjoy it."

My cock, already hardening against her curvy ass, pulses.

"You sure you can handle what I want from you, Greer?"

She reaches up and curves her hand around my head. "I think the real question is whether you can handle what

I want from you."

"Anything you want, I'm your man."

She tugs at the short hair at the back. "Anything?"

At this point in my life, I'm closer to being able to give her anything than I've ever been before. And when she looks at me like this, there's nothing I could deny her.

"Yeah, baby. Anything."

She wiggles her ass in my lap and presses her lips to my jaw. If I kiss her right now, there's a good chance that I'm going to fuck her in the backseat of this car, and that's not something I'm willing to have an audience for. Especially not her driver, who is just about to pull open the door.

Thank fuck we're only ten minutes from her building.

"Can you make it quick, Ed?"

"Of course, sir."

Ed, the trusty driver, looks at me with Greer on my lap in the rearview mirror. I see the look of judgment before he schools his expression. Big Brother is probably going to be receiving a full report as soon as Ed drops us off.

I may not have all the money Creighton Karas does, but I'm not opposed to going toe-to-toe with the guy. Or I could just kidnap Greer and take her away to some remote island and keep her there until she's as addicted to me as I am to her, and her brother's opinion ceases to matter. As far as I know, she never told him about me before, because I never received a death threat from his camp.

We pull up in front of the building, and Ed hops out and opens the door. I slide out of the car, lifting Greer as I stand, readjusting her in my arms.

Her quick intake of breath signals her surprise. She grips my shoulders tighter, her gaze clashing with mine.

"I'm not gonna let you fall."

"I can walk. I'm not that drunk." Her protest is quiet and halfhearted at best.

"And I want you in my arms, so I'm carrying you." I nod at Ed, who is watching us with eagle eyes. "Good night, sir. Thank you for the ride."

"Of course, Mr. Westman. Have a good evening."

I can tell he wants to tell me something else, probably to warn me that I'd better take good care of Greer, but he stays silent.

He doesn't need to worry. I'm not going to let anything happen to her. I'm capable of protecting her at least as well as he is, and probably better. After all, I've got more than money and fear of Creighton Karas motivating me.

Greer waves to the doorman as we head inside. His polite chin raise gives away none of his true thoughts about watching me carry her through the foyer. For a moment, I wonder if this is something he's seen before, or if he's really that good at hiding his shock.

"You get carried up to your apartment a lot?"

Greer's laugh is muffled by my shirt as I elbow the call button for the elevator. "Nope. This is a first for me. I don't think Tristan could've actually picked me up. Maybe that's why he was always encouraging me to lose weight."

I already wanted to fuck up this Tristan punk, but even more so now at Greer's confession.

"Was he mentally defective? What the fuck was the guy's problem?"

Greer shrugs against my chest as we step inside the elevator and the silver doors glide closed. "He sucked. I'm glad I didn't let him fuck me in the ass. He could have that redheaded ho for that."

"Whoa. What?"

She looks up at me, blinking. "That's what I walked in on. Him fucking a redhead in the ass. She was actually quite polite about the whole thing. Told me I should've just let him have at it because you could hardly tell." She lowers her voice to a stage whisper. "He suffered from pencil-dick-itis. I only got off if I got myself off. God, that's pathetic."

Well, at least I know I've got that fucker beat in more than one department. There's nothing pencil-like about my dick, and I know how to make Greer come.

"And you stayed with him because . . ." I let my question trail off. I don't want to talk about this prick, but my curiosity is strong.

Greer shifts in my hold as the elevator slows to a stop and the doors slide open. Her voice is quiet when she finally answers. "I don't give up. I'm not a quitter. I thought it would get better if I kept working at it. Trying new things. But it didn't get better. I guess I owe him a thank-you for cutting it off because I didn't know how to pull the trigger. After I got over the rage and hurt, it was more a relief than anything."

I hate that she went through that shit, but I'm also really fucking happy she's not still attached to the guy and nursing a broken heart.

"Anyway, I don't want to talk about him." She turns

her face up to mine, her lips curving mischievously. "I want to talk about all the dirty things you're going to do to me, and how hard you're going to make me come."

CHAPTER
THIRTEEN

Greer

I should be blushing at the things I'm saying to Cav, but something about him destroys my filters. This level of need surging through me is unique to him—totally raw and primal.

I know my words have an effect on Cav because his voice is rough when he says, "Keys, baby. We get inside this apartment, and I'm going to tell you exactly what I'm gonna do to you."

I dig into the bag slung over my shoulder and fish out my keys. Cav makes short work of getting inside. He doesn't stop once the door is closed behind us, but instead of heading into the bedroom like I thought he would, he goes toward the kitchen.

"What—"

"No more questions, Greer. I'm going to give you what

you want, and you're gonna love it."

My feet touch the floor and before I realize what he's doing, I'm spinning around and bending until my forehead touches the bar level of my countertop.

Cav wraps my hands around the edges. "Don't let go." He leans close, his big body covering mine as he speaks low into my ear. "You're not going to let go until you've come at least twice, and even then, not until I say. Yesterday was just a warm-up, baby girl. It's time for you to understand exactly what I like."

Shivers ripple across my skin, and my nipples harden against the cool granite. Heat pools between my legs, and I'm on edge waiting for him. I was perfectly honest in the car earlier; I'm drunk enough to lose my inhibitions, but not too drunk not to know what I'm doing and appreciate it.

Tonight in the bar, his presence reinforced something I knew three years ago—Cav is more man than any I've ever met.

He steps back, separating the press of his body from mine, but his hands never leave me. Starting at my fingertips, which are wrapped around the edge of the counter, he drags his palms down my arms, pulling up the sleeves of my light sweater.

"Softest skin I've ever touched. Like silk." His voice is husky and every word sounds like a revelation. "This is coming off."

He grasps the sweater at the hem and peels it up my torso, and I lift just enough for him to slide it the rest of the way free. Underneath it I have nothing but a bra. Lacy and black, with an array of straps at the back forming a starburst pattern.

"Every damn thing about you screams expensive. It doesn't matter what you wear, what you do, how you do it, you're all class." His lips press to my shoulder. "And you're all mine. You're gonna be my dirty girl."

Another round of shivers skate down my spine as goose bumps rise along my skin. I've been waiting years for this moment, and I'm going to enjoy it completely.

Cav smooths his hands down my sides until he reaches my waist. My black skirt isn't indecently short, but it's not exactly long either. It's a kilt style, and when Cav unhooks the fastenings, it drops away. The cheeky panties I have on beneath leave enough to the imagination not to be scandalous if a gust of wind happens to blow up my skirt. I think about these things because it has totally happened to me in the city more than once.

"Next time you wear this skirt with me, you're not wearing panties, and I'm going to make you come while we're in a room full of people."

I arch into the palm of his hand as it cups my ass. The heat disappears and a sharp *crack* against my left cheek comes next.

I gasp in shock, but Cav silences me.

"Quiet. That's me showing you what's gonna happen if you wear this skirt and no panties without me. I'll lay you out over this counter and spank this perfect little ass until you understand that it belongs to me and only me."

I should rail against his caveman comment, but I can't. My panties, the ones he's trailing a finger along the edge of, are soaked.

I've read books about men like this. Dominant ones who take what they want and give mind-blowing orgasms to their women, but the overabundance of stuffed-shirt bankers and lawyers in my life made me believe they didn't actually exist. But they do. And one is sliding my panties down over my ass and letting them drop to the floor.

"Step out of them."

I comply, but Cav isn't done giving orders.

"Spread your legs." When I inch my feet apart, he isn't satisfied. "Wider."

Feeling ridiculously exposed, I slide my foot another inch to the side. It still isn't enough for Cav. He lowers himself to his knees and wraps a hand around my ankle, moving my foot where he wants it.

I want him. More than I've ever wanted any man before.

"Look at this pretty cunt, all wet for me. Fuck, you're beautiful. Smooth and slick. You're going to ride my face until you scream, and then I'm going to fill you full of my hard cock."

His words unleash another wave of heat within me. If he doesn't put his mouth on me *now,* I'll grab his head and put him where I want him. Instantly, I wonder if I would end up with a few more strikes across my burning ass as punishment. I bite my lip at the thought. No one has ever spanked me before . . . and it was hot. I'm tempted to do exactly what he said to get him to do it again.

My thoughts derail as Cav's palms slide up my inner thighs, stopping just short of where I want him. "I like you like this. Wet. Bare. Waiting for me like a good girl to take whatever I give you. Fuck, I've been thinking about this for years. What you taste like. How hot this pussy is going to be once I get my mouth on it."

"Are you trying to make me beg?" I ask, my tone so husky, my voice doesn't sound like me.

Cav's chuckle is dark as his breath brushes my inner thighs. "When I want you to beg, you'll know it."

Those are the last words he speaks before he repositions himself between my legs and his hands palm my ass, spreading me wide. His lips graze my clit and my muscles clench deliciously. When his mouth closes over me, I can't hold back a moan.

After a few teasing circles and licks, I'm already pressing down on his face. Cav doesn't waste time—or let me dictate his movements. He's devouring me, swirling my clit, eating me like I'm his favorite dessert. And I want to be.

My fingers grip the counter as he fucks me with his tongue, and I writhe against his mouth. My slickness must be dripping on him, and he increases the pressure, pulling me more firmly against his mouth. I do exactly what he told me I would do—ride his face.

My orgasm is close. I've never come this quickly before . . . actually, I've never come from oral sex *ever*. But Cav's dominant words and his commanding and skilled performance are about to change that.

And when one thumb slides across my ass to *that spot*, something inside me splinters. Untried nerve endings flare to life at the pressure of his thumb on my ass.

"Oh my God. Oh my God. What—"

My nipples harden even further as the pleasure center in my brain shifts into overdrive. Too many sensations, and the orgasm explodes with the scream from my lungs.

Cav doesn't stop. The pressure on my ass intensifies, forcing the waves of my orgasm to continue ripping through my body. I'm shaking, hands gripping the edge of the counter like it'll help me hold on to my sanity. I open my mouth to plead for something, what I'm not sure, when he pulls away and stands behind me.

His hands caress my arms, skimming across my sensitized skin until they close over my fingers. Lowering his head, he nips my earlobe between his teeth. "You did good, baby girl. You're still holding on. But you're not gonna let go until you scream for me twice, are you?"

"Not letting go." I want to scream for him twice. I want more of this body-shaking pleasure he's given me. Seeking more contact, I push my ass into the erection pressing against me.

Cav keeps talking, his tone seductive and slow. "You liked my thumb on your ass. You're gonna take a hell of a lot more there. I'm gonna stretch you out until you can take my cock."

Shivers chase down my spine as I release a small moan against the counter. I want him and all the forbidden things he says he's going to give me.

"But not tonight. Tonight I'm gonna fuck this tight little pussy again. You know why?"

"Why?" I whisper.

"Because it's mine. It was made for my cock. Every guy

in that bar wanted to be me tonight, and it didn't have jack shit to do with who I am. They all wanted to be the guy taking you home and fucking you tonight. But they can't have you because I'm not letting you go again. Do you understand me?" Every word rings with the distinct sound of possession.

I try to nod, but my cheek against the counter doesn't allow it.

"Answer me, Greer."

"Yes." Right now, I'd say anything he wanted to hear. I need him inside me.

"Good girl." He releases his grip on my hands. "Don't move."

Once again, his touch is all I can focus on as his palms follow the curves of my body. I love how he handles me so confidently—no question of whether I'm going to enjoy what he's going to give me.

His hands disappear and the sound of his zipper and the rustle of his jeans meet my ears. My anticipation ratchets up a dozen notches when he slides his cock between my legs and teases me with the head.

"Hope you're ready, baby." He presses against my entrance and sinks to the hilt with a single thrust.

I moan against the counter, my fingers uncurling and clenching where he told me to hold on. Filled. Taken. Owned. All of these feelings riot inside me as he fucks me with sharp drives of his hips, slowing for a few and then fucking me harder.

My fingers twitch with the urge to reach down and touch my clit, ensuring my orgasm will hit me fast and hard, but I keep my hold, trying to obey. Something about wanting to touch myself but knowing I can't sends me higher, hotter, faster.

Cav's big hand comes around my hip, and he centers the heel against the spot that's dying for pressure. I bite my lip to keep from screaming. It's a lost cause.

The orgasm hits me hard, and I squeeze the counter until my fingers go numb and my body vibrates. Cav doesn't slow, his thrusts continuing to pound into me.

"Fuuuuck." His bellowing roar echoes in my apartment as his cock jerks inside me.

Our heaving breaths and thundering heartbeats fill the ensuing silence.

He reaches up and sweeps his thumb across my knuckles. "You can let go now, baby girl."

His lips press against my hair as I uncurl my fingers. I stretch them a few times until Cav takes over—rubbing each joint until the ache fades. When he's done, he reaches for the box of tissues tucked into the corner of my counter and pulls away. I snag a couple, use them to clean up, and turn to face him.

What do I do now? What do I say? Are we together? Do I want us to be together? Do I trust him? My brain has kicked into logical mode and the questions are bombarding me.

He told me I was his, but for how long? Until he loses interest in whatever we're doing? He's not staying in New York forever. His life is in LA.

Dammit, why can't the postcoital bliss stage last longer for me? Why can't I be the girl who rolls with the casual sex and doesn't ask questions?

Wait. Why can't I do that? Nothing's stopping me. I can be that girl. I don't have to let my emotions get involved. I can take whatever this is for what it's worth, enjoy it, and still keep my heart intact.

Decision made, I give myself an internal nod of approval. No emotions. No heart. Just casual sex while I see where this goes. And if that casual sex happens to be the best I've ever had . . . then all the better for me.

Winning, Greer. You are winning.

"Well, um. Thanks. That was . . . a perfect nightcap. I better crash. I've got a lot to get done tomorrow. Have a good night."

I keep my tone light and casual, and Cav stares at me like I've grown another head. I want to fidget under the intensity of his gaze, especially because I'm standing here naked except for my bra and heels, but I keep my hands locked together in front of me. *Casual. Cool. Calm. Collected.* I may be none of those things right now, but I'm sure as hell going to fake it until I make it.

"Then I'll . . . see you tomorrow," he says slowly, as though he's trying to form a sentence in a foreign language.

"If I can carve out some time, I'll, um, shoot you a text?" I don't even have his number.

He shakes his head, his eyes narrowed. "I'll find you, Greer." His expression is calling me out on my bullshit blowoff. Like he knows what game I'm playing, and he's better at it.

That just hardens my resolve. This is my life. Not a game.

"Good night, Cav. Thanks again."

He leans in, and I expect another kiss on my forehead or my cheek, but Cav is having none of it. He buries his hand in my hair, gripping the back of my head, and covers my lips with his. His tongue slides inside, no permission requested or needed.

I'm still catching up with the devouring kiss when he releases me and steps away.

"Good night, Greer. My pleasure."

CHAPTER
FOURTEEN

Greer

"The kitchen counter? Nice. You're going to have to point out that space so I don't accidentally sit where you almost lost your anal cherry."

I consider hanging up on Banner because the last thing I want to talk about is my anal cherry, but . . . I've been dishing with her for years about her hot sexcapades and my lukewarm ones. Now that I've finally got something to share, I'm *sharing*.

"Right side, between the last two bar stools."

"Damn . . . So, was it as good as the first time? Even though you weren't banging against any walls?"

I don't hesitate. "Better. He's *good*. Like, maybe best ever."

She sighs. "I don't know if that means he's off-the-charts incredible, or whether I should send a sympathy bouquet to you for all the years of shitty sex you've had."

"I like flowers," I say offhandedly. "I don't get them often enough. Or ever. Unless I buy them myself." Now that I think about it, that's pretty tragic. I make a mental note to buy myself flowers more often because, dammit, I deserve them and spectacular sex.

"Well, shit, this guy better get on the ball if he wants to impress you, then. Too bad he hasn't been in any romcoms. That flower-giving shit would be ingrained."

"That's not what this is."

"What do you mean? That your life isn't a funny/sexy movie? Because it could be. Although right now you're heading into porn territory. I mean, how much of a story line was there before you banged against the door?"

"Seriously, shut up. You know what I mean. This thing with Cav, it's not real. It's not going to last. I don't know what game he's playing, but considering his track record for following through with me, I'm not going to expect anything but hot sex. That's fair, right?"

There's a moment of silence on the line. "One time does not a track record make," Banner says.

"Yeah, okay, so he stood me up once. *For three years. Without a word.* That's bullshit and you know it. I'm not going to get all hearts and flowers over him now because I can't trust it. And even if I could trust it, I don't need to be all hearts and flowers over anyone. I just got out of a two-year relationship that sucked."

Hindsight is a brilliant thing. Why I stayed with Tristan for as long as I did, existing on scraps of attention, admittedly shitty sex, and me doing all the work to keep some semblance of a relationship going, I'll never know. What a waste of my time.

"I know. I tried to tell you Tristan was a D-bag, but you didn't want to hear it from anyone. But guess what? If Cav is a D-bag, I'll tell you. At least he'd be a D-bag that makes you come and is built like a fucking brick shithouse. Seriously, I kind of hate you right now. I want to climb on and ride that ride."

My inner claws come out with a wave of possessiveness I don't expect. "No one's riding that ride but me until I'm done with it."

"Then own that shit, girl. Millions of women would kill to be in your position, not to mention trying to get knocked up with his kid so they've got a hold on him for life. You're wasting opportunities right and left."

I cringe when she says *knocked up*. "Shit. I forgot to tell you. We didn't use a condom. He wasn't freaked out at all. I need to get checked for everything under the sun now, don't I?" A loud *whack* sounds in my ear from the other end. "What was that?"

"Sorry, dropped my phone. You're telling me Mr. Hollywood didn't wrap it up? Are you serious? That's criminally stupid for a man in his position. Unless . . ." She trails off meaningfully.

"Unless what?"

"Maybe he wants you knocked up. Maybe he's the one looking for a hold on you. For real. Long-term shit. You're a catch, Greer."

I shove my palm out into the air in front of me, even though Banner can't see it. "Stop. Stop right there. We're not talking about that possibility. I'm baby-proof and that's not changing. He didn't knock me up."

"But you've fucked twice, no condom, and he didn't freak out."

"Mm-hmm. That's what I said."

Silence hangs on the line for a few beats. "That's just weird. It's like Famous Dude 101 to ward off the gold diggers."

"That's what I told him!" My hand flails wildly, and I'm happy no one is here to see my crazy gestures.

"And?"

"He really wasn't concerned."

"That doesn't make sense. I bet his agent would be concerned . . . or maybe not, because you've already got plenty of money and there's no way you're after his. I guess that makes you the safest chick out there to come in."

I scrunch up my face. "Ugh. I'm done with this conversation."

"Maybe you should start drinking. That's when the interesting stuff happens."

"It's noon."

"Which isn't too early to talk about whether or not you're going to let him pop that last cherry."

Banner's been selling me on anal sex since prep school. I think part of me has been holding out this long just because she's been equal parts blasé and overly gung ho about it. When Tristan brought it up casually, I shut him down completely. Even then, I think I knew I couldn't trust him with every part of me. And I don't care what anyone says, letting someone put something *in* your *out* hole takes a hell of a lot of trust.

"Look, Greer. You're a catch—the shit, if you will. If you're finally going to take the D up the B, it needs to be a good and memorable experience. Chances are Cav Westman is used to having women throw every part of their bodies at him, so he's got what it takes to make this good for you. And if it sucks, when we're old ladies rolling around in our scooters wearing velour tracksuits, we'll be reliving the time you got butt-fucked by a movie star. There's virtually no downside here."

Tears trickle down my cheeks as laughter racks my body. "Wow, B. I don't even—"

"Just say you're going for it and you'll give me all the dirty—pun intended—details after the deed is done."

"I'm making no promises on the former, but if I go for it, you'll definitely get the latter."

"Deal."

The next call I receive isn't nearly so entertaining.

"Greer, what the hell is going on?"

Creighton's harsh tone surprises me. I thought we were all good finally.

"Well, hello to you too, Crey. How's life on the road?"

"Have you seen yourself on damn near every gossip site out there this morning?"

"Actually, I haven't." And I'm surprised Banner hasn't seen them or mentioned them either. But then again, she's working her tail off today, and other than our little lunchtime chat, she's swamped at work.

"My entire PR team was already working overtime to try to crush the ad, and now they're bombarded with pictures of you and some actor. I need some goddamned details so they can spin it. Who the fuck is this guy to you?"

It's a question I dreaded having to answer years ago because I knew Creighton would never understand dating someone so far outside our social circle. Before Holly, at least. I stick to the truth as much as I can.

"He's an old friend. We met when I was at Columbia."

"Why didn't I know about this?"

"Because you were happily minding your own business and letting me live my own life."

A deep sound of frustration comes through the line. "And now your stunts are impacting my life and my business, Greer. I thought you understood that. Investor confidence is taking another hit with this stuff."

Guilt floods me, twisting in my stomach. "I'm sorry, Crey. I didn't think about that. But I'm also not going to live my life any differently just to appease investors. You haven't, so why should the rules be any different for me?"

"The rules are different, whether you want them to be or not. I'm having the head of PR call you to walk through the dos and don'ts you need to be observing now that you've got this guy in the mix. Lay low; don't attract any more media attention. And I've got a team digging into his background. I need to know exactly who we're dealing with before you see him again."

And once again, I'm a wayward teenager who can't possibly be trusted to know what I want or what's best for me.

"Call them off." My voice is flat and filled with determination.

"Not a chance in hell."

"You don't need to dig into him. I know exactly who he is and what he's about."

"Greer—"

I decide to lay it all out. "I'm already sleeping with him, Crey. Whatever you find out, it's not affecting what I'm going to do. So basically, quit wasting your time."

"You're more stubborn than I am." His voice twists into a familiar growl.

"I learned from the best."

"Look, Greer, I need to know he's not trying to scam you. You know what you've got to offer, and I'm not saying he's looking for an easy payday, but I'd be a shitty brother if I wasn't watching out for you."

"I know, but I'm also not going to marry the guy like you married some perfect stranger after a one-night stand. So, quit worrying so much. If those pictures of us are already stirring interest, then the paps are going to be around whether I lay low or not. I might as well enjoy myself."

"If stock prices keep falling in response, I'll be taking action whether you like it or not. That's a promise."

The threat clearly on the table, Creighton and I say our good-byes and hang up. My life has never been simple, and today is no exception.

Is it worth it? For the non-relationship I have with Cav?

I have no answer to that question, except I'm not ready to call it off yet.

CHAPTER
FIFTEEN

Cav

As I wrap Greer's hand around the grip of a gun, I wonder if I'm making a huge mistake.

But where do you take the girl who has everything on a date? If you're me, you take her to the gun range for a dual-purpose date—Greer gets to see that I've got mad skills, and she learns something useful.

"So I just pull the trigger," she yells, her voice abnormally loud because of the ear-protection effect.

"Squeeze," I tell her. "It's a smooth motion." I demonstrate with my finger as she bites her lip and concentrates downrange at the target.

It's been a thirty-minute crash course in gun safety, and we're finally getting to the fun part. At least, I hope she thinks it's the fun part.

She squeezes the trigger but doesn't jump at the percussion. Good sign. There's no hole in the target, so I know she missed.

"Try again. Aim a little lower."

She squeezes the trigger again, this time putting a hole in the chest of the yellow man hanging in the lane downrange. Greer flips the safety on, sets the gun down on the counter, and yanks off her ear protection.

"I did it!" Clapping her hands and bouncing, she looks younger than twenty-six and too damn innocent to drag into my life. But that doesn't mean I won't.

"Damn good job, baby girl. You want to give it another shot?"

She glances from me to the black 9mm Sig Sauer. "Sure, why not?"

"You've got plenty of ammo, so you might as well use it up."

"Okay. Let's do this." Excitement lights up her face, and a triumphant feeling grows in my chest.

Once her ear protection is back in place, she unloads the remainder of the rounds in the magazine, and I reload it for her. Once she's put a suitable number of holes in the target, she lays the gun down again, her dark eyes dancing with enthusiasm.

"I want to see you shoot, Hollywood."

I grin at her nickname for me and crowd her against the wall of the booth of our shooting lane. The rest of the room is empty because I bought out the entire range for a couple of hours so we could have some privacy.

"Hollywood, huh?" I lean down, teasing both of us with the promise of my lips on hers.

Greer's palms skim up my chest and she clasps her hands behind my neck. "Seems appropriate," she whispers, her voice turning husky.

"I'll let you call me whatever you want right now, baby. But when I'm inside you tonight, I want you moaning my name."

"I guess we'll have to see if you can make that happen."

"It's a guarantee, not a possibility."

"So you say."

"So I know."

"Are you going to tease me or kiss me?" she asks.

"Whatever I want—that's what I'm always gonna do."

And right now I want her smile, not just her mouth. I want that warmth and energy radiating from her. Shit, I just want her. Everything she is, and I want her more than I've wanted anything in my life. I will not waste this second chance I've been given. But if I fuck it up, I will steal a third chance. And a fourth. Whatever it takes, and regardless of whether I deserve it.

But Greer is sick of waiting for me to make my move, and yanks my head down to her level and takes the kiss I'm teasing her with.

I take control, cupping her jaw and tilting her head to the side. My knee slides between her legs and she presses against it. A quick fuck in the gun range sounds like a hell of a plan—until my phone buzzes in my pocket. I ignore it, but it starts again.

Pulling away, I glance at the screen. BLOCKED CALL. The list of people with this number is short, which leaves me with few possibilities, some of them better than others.

"I gotta take this, baby," I say, stepping back. "It'll only take a few minutes." She's eying the gun as I swipe the screen. "And don't shoot anything until I'm back."

Rolling her eyes, Greer turns around and begins pulling in the target.

I step out of the room before I speak. "You got me. What do you want?"

The voice on the other end is all too familiar. "You know what I want, Cav."

CHAPTER

SIXTEEN

Greer

As soon as Cav leaves my sight, I pull out my phone. My notifications are blowing up.

Bad sign.

Two missed calls from Creighton and two texts. A text from Holly. Two from Banner.

I type in my passcode and read through the messages.

CREIGHTON: *This is NOT laying low.*

CREIGHTON: *Answer your fucking phone.*

CREIGHTON: *I'm sending Cannon.*

HOLLY: *Cav Westman is totally hot, but your brother is losing his shit. You *might* want to answer.*

BANNER: *You're my hero. Top post on CelebSightingsNYC. Oh, and according to the gossip sites, you're officially a couple.*

BANNER: You look hot in that pic, BTW.

Do I want to see what they're all talking about? Of course. Who wouldn't?

I tap on my browser and google CelebSightingsNYC and Cav's name. Sure enough, the first pic that pops up is us getting out of a cab in front of the shooting range. That fucking cabbie. It's the only explanation that makes sense with the angle of the picture.

I need to get Cav so we can get the hell out of here before the vultures descend. I mean, I'm not saying we're the most interesting news story in the city tonight, but we're probably toward the top of the list. *And* everyone knows where we are.

I leave the gun on the counter and slip around the corner to where I hear his deep voice. I'm not trying to eavesdrop, but I do wonder if it's his agent or manager, or someone else calling to give him the heads-up that we've been spotted.

"No, I'm done. Not going back there." Cav's tone is harsh. "Fine. I'm out." He hangs up and strides toward the door, his head jerking up when he sees me standing in the doorway.

I lift my phone and point to the screen. "Cover's blown, Hollywood. We're being celeb-watched. My phone is blowing up. Is that what your call was about?"

Cav shakes his head. "No. What happened?" He takes my phone and reads the screen before it starts vibrating in his hand.

"Your brother," he says, handing it back.

"Shit, he's called three times. He told me to lay low and let all this stuff blow over, so he's not happy with me right now . . ." The phone keeps vibrating as I explain.

"Are you going to answer it?"

"Mmm . . . I don't want to." I consider it again, knowing I've only got a few more seconds to decide. "I guess I better."

I swipe the screen and answer with, "Don't yell at me."

"Greer," Creighton's deep voice rumbles with frustration. "I thought we had an understanding."

"You told me to lay low and I'm laying low," I counter.

"Then why is your picture on the top of every gossip site? The ad is front and center again, and Holly tells me you're fucking trending on Twitter."

My stomach twists, feeling weighed down with all of the bullets I just shot. "Shit. Really?" Trending on Twitter isn't exactly where I want to be.

"Apparently the citizens of New York are turning this into a fun-filled fiasco. You need to get the hell out of town and *really* lay low."

"My apartment—"

Creighton cuts me off. "Is being watched around the clock because it's been leaked that Cav bought a unit there too."

"So, what do we do? Go to LA?" I cut my eyes to Cav when I realize I just made us a *we* and offered up his residence as a solution.

"No, Cannon is on his way. He'll take you to Teterboro, and you're getting out of the country for a while. I've got a friend with a place in Belize, and he's agreed to let you stay as long as you need. Since you're lacking a job, that shouldn't be a big deal."

Say what? "Seriously? I need to pack if I'm going—"

"He and his wife leave a full wardrobe at the house, and you're close to her size. He's a big bastard, so Cav should be fine. Just get in the SUV when Cannon pulls up, and get the fuck out of town so I can clean up this mess before it becomes a full-blown situation."

There are plenty of times when I want to argue with my brother, but I'm not sure this is one of them. There's something in his tone that tells me to choose my fight carefully. I feel like there's more going on here than what Creighton is telling me, which wouldn't be all that surprising. I trust him, though, and if he tells me to go, I'll go.

"Okay. If that's what you think is best."

"Good. Cannon just texted that he's a few blocks away."

"Sorry, Crey. I didn't mean for this to happen . . ."

"I know. Now, do what Cannon tells you and I'll be in touch."

I hang up and Cav is waiting semi-patiently. His jaw is tense and his hands are clenched into fists. "Your brother's sending you away, and you're going to let him." The words carry a strong dose of fury.

"He's sending *us* away. If you're game, that is. How do you feel about Belize?"

Cav's brows draw together deeper. "Belize? What the hell?"

I fill him in on Creighton's directive that I lay low, and give him the details of the conversation that he didn't overhear. The muscles of his jaw relax and so do his fists.

"Cannon should be here any minute to take us to Teterboro."

"You're sure you want to do this?"

"Run away to a tropical paradise with you? My brother has certainly had worse ideas."

Cav finally smiles and grabs my hand. "Then let's get a move on."

We return the gun to the counter and make our way out to the street. Before I can look for Cannon, I'm blinded by flashing cameras. *Damn paparazzi.* Cav pulls me into his side, and we push through the crowd as the questions start flying.

"Cav, is it true that you answered Greer's ad? Did you meet all the requirements?"

"Are you a couple?"

"When's the quickie wedding like Creighton and Holly?"

The last thing I want to do is address any of them. Why? Because I don't have any answers. Cav, it seems, isn't plagued by the same problem. He stops and faces the crowd.

"Cannon is right here," I whisper as the window of an SUV rolls down and he shouts my name.

"This will only take a second," Cav replies. To the flashing cameras, he says, "If you had this amazing woman on your arm, wouldn't you do everything you could to make her happy and keep her in your life? I don't plan on letting her get away."

The door to the SUV pops open and Cannon motions me inside. I tug at Cav's arm and he follows.

"Better go find another story to chase, guys. That's all you're going to get out of us tonight."

We both slide inside the SUV, and Cav slams the door as the questions continue to come.

From his seat beside me, Cannon says, "Was that really necessary? This is the start of you *laying low*. Feeding the press sound bites isn't necessary. Let our PR people craft a statement, and we'll leave it at that."

Cav, on my left, faces Cannon, and I'm caught between two big men, one dark and the other light. When I first met him, I crushed on Cannon, but as I got older, I knew I could never feel that way about a man who was almost as close to me as my brother.

"I think I've got PR down. You do realize this isn't the first time I've been chased by paps, right? In LA, you get this kind of bullshit when you go out for coffee."

Cannon lays a hand on my knee. "Well, it's not everyday bullshit for Greer, and you're not helping matters when it comes to salvaging her reputation. Unlike yours, which is for purely entertainment value, her reputation matters to investors who need to have confidence in the Karas family and all they represent. I don't expect some former janitor to understand how that works."

"Maintenance man." Cav's tone is dark. "And I get how it works. I'm not looking to do anything but help Greer, so you can back the fuck off." He wraps his arm around my shoulders and pulls me closer to his side.

Cannon can't mistake the possessive gesture, and neither can I. I just hope we can get to the jet without these two coming to blows.

CHAPTER
SEVENTEEN

Cav

That fucking prick Cannon leaves us at the corporate aviation building, and another driver takes us out to the tarmac where we climb onto the black Karas International jet. When I flew in here, I had visions of taking Greer on my own jet and flying her somewhere to impress her.

I forgot for an instant that I'm dealing with a woman who has probably never flown commercial, and a private jet is just another normal thing in her life. *What can I give her that she's never had before?* That's the question running through my mind as the flight attendant returns with our drinks and a few snacks. Greer knocks back her gin and tonic like it's water.

"You okay, baby?"

She was quiet the entire ride out to the airport while

Cannon and I shot daggers at each other. Her silence sets me on edge. Has she decided that getting pulled into the press because of me isn't worth it? *Fuck.* I'm not letting her go now, so we're going to have to find a way to deal with this.

Running away to a tropical paradise only works as a temporary solution. And honestly, I don't understand why her reputation is so important to the investors of her brother's companies.

"Greer, you okay?" I ask again because my last question received no answer. She's lost in her thoughts, but my words finally penetrate.

She uncurls her fingers from around the tumbler, only to squeeze them tight again. "I'm fine. Just . . . thinking about how crazy my life is becoming. I went from working sixteen or eighteen hours a day at the firm to being unemployed, and now this. The last few days have been kind of surreal, and I'm still processing."

"Do you want to go back?" The captain is just beginning to taxi down the runway, so any decisions need to be made right now.

She shakes her head. "No. I really don't want to go back. That's the part I'm trying not to feel guilty about."

I wrap my arm around her shoulders and press a kiss to her temple. "Why would you feel guilty?"

"Because running makes me look like an irresponsible jet-setting little princess when that's not who I am and it never will be." She pauses for a moment before adding, "But I'm greedy because this means that I get to run away with you and leave the world behind. We don't have to deal with all the bullshit for a few days, and can just have fun."

I wish she added something about figuring out what's going on between us and how this relationship is going to work, but I'm getting the message loud and clear that Greer isn't ready for that. She's not going to admit we have a relationship or a future.

That's too damn bad because when I came back into her life, I did it with the intention of making this a permanent change. She's going to have to find a way to deal with it because I'm not letting her go. Not this time.

Instead of pushing the issue, I lean closer and press another kiss to her temple. It's becoming a habit that will be impossible to break.

"Let's take this one day at a time and see what happens. I've got nowhere else I need to be, and I can't think of anything I'd like better than you in a bikini on the beach before we go back to our room and I strip you naked and make you scream my name."

Greer turns her body into me and lays her head on my shoulder. "I think I can handle that."

"You don't have a choice."

I'm not sure what to expect from the very minimal description of the place Greer gave me, but when we land on an airstrip I'm not even sure is paved, I'm even more intrigued. The billionaire badass big brother wouldn't send his treasured and protected little sister anywhere less than the best, though.

Three years ago, I dreamed of being able to steal her away for some extravagant vacation to impress her, and now we've been handed this golden opportunity. Greer once told me she wanted to be wooed, and now I've got a secluded tropical paradise and no paparazzi.

Game on.

A man in a golf cart waits just beyond the runway and waves us over. He smiles and holds up a handwritten sign that reads GREER.

"Bags?" he asks, looking somewhat confused at our empty hands.

"Not this time," I reply.

"Okay then. Let's get you to the house."

I wrap an arm around Greer as we climb onto the backseat of the golf cart. The headlights cut through the pitch-black darkness ahead of us as he drives us along a rutted and bumpy road that appears to be packed sand. Dozens of blue crabs skitter to the sides of the street as the light touches them.

Where the hell are we?

Less than five minutes later, he slows at a black metal gate connecting two white concrete walls. There's a keypad, and he inputs a long combination before the gate slides to one side.

"I'm Juan, the caretaker here." He gestures to a small cottage that sits close to the cement wall and gate. "I'll be available if you need me. My wife, Rea, cooks and cleans. So if you have any special requests, just let her know." He pats his belly. "She's one of the best cooks on the island, so you're in for a treat."

"Island? I thought we were in Belize?" Greer asks.

Juan's hearty laugh shakes his belly, and he's probably putting us in the category of *stupid American tourists*.
"You are in Belize. Welcome to Caye Caulker. We're the
second largest island in the country, but don't be fooled,
there's not far to go. You're at the south end now; the village is at the north end of this section, before the Split."

"The Split?" I ask, wondering what the hell he's talking
about.

"A channel where Hurricane Hattie ripped the island
in half back in '61. You'll see it. There are more houses
on the other side, but you need a boat to get there. We
have one, and I can take you wherever you want to go.
I don't recommend taking it yourself because navigating
the reef is tricky unless you've been doing it for years. But
anything you want—snorkel, scuba, fishing, exploring the
cays, I'll take you."

Greer and I both thank him as he leads us toward the
large white concrete house on concrete pilings. Ornate
yellow tiled stairs lead us to a wide porch that looks like it
wraps around the place. Juan removes keys from his pocket, unlocks the door, and hands them to me.

"I'll leave you to explore. You'll see Rea in the morning. What time would you like breakfast?"

I glance at Greer and raise an eyebrow, indicating it's
her call.

"Eight o'clock would be fine. Thank you, Juan. Have a
good night."

I shut and lock the white wood door behind us and

watch Greer as she spins in a circle in the large entryway. High ceilings are lined in dark wood with exposed beams, and the walls are painted a vivid yellow that matches the blue, green, red, and yellow mosaic tiles patterned across the floor.

It's everything you'd expect from a tropical beach house. A round wood table sits in the middle of the entryway with a huge vase of vibrant, fresh flowers. From this vantage, I can see a large sectional in the living room, a matching wood coffee table, and a flat-screen television mounted on the wall. Bright canvases line the walls, adding color beyond the yellow. Thin white curtains blow in the breeze along the entire wall of windows facing the ocean. Waves crash just outside in the darkness.

Greer completes her circle, and I wait for her reaction. She's probably been on countless luxury vacations, making this place nothing special. Hell, maybe even quaint. By my standards, and from what I've seen so far, it's a pretty sweet pad, one I'd be happy to call my own.

"I love it," Greer says, her voice quiet. "It's so perfect."

"Let's check it out."

With a grin, I follow her from the entryway into the living room, and then the dining room and kitchen. The kitchen has dark wood cabinets, black-and-gray granite countertops, and stainless appliances. It's just as nice as the setup at my place in LA, but the vibrant colors of the walls, art, and backsplash give it a strong island vibe.

We venture back through the living room and find three bedrooms, the largest of which is clearly the master. A large wood four-poster sits at one end, facing a wall of windows with billowing curtains. The east side of the room is also lined with windows, leading me to believe we're going to see a hell of a sunrise.

I gotta hand it to Creighton Karas, this place is perfect. Fuck, it feels like a place you'd carry a bride across a threshold on a honeymoon.

I shut that thought down. Greer isn't ready, and I'm not going to freak her out by talking about serious shit. In fact, my mission with this trip? Get her so fucking addicted to my body and my cock that she never wants another man again. Once I've accomplished that goal, I'll move on to the next phase of my plan.

I stop at the doorway of the bathroom as Greer steps inside. "Damn, this place is perfect." I take in the giant tiled shower and mammoth tub. They're going to get plenty of use.

"Totally perfect."

As Greer turns back to me, I take in her appearance. She's as beautiful as ever, but dark circles are making an appearance under her eyes. She's dead on her feet. Neither of us slept on the six-hour flight; instead, we checked out most of the gossip sites that had posted our pictures. We left each other to our thoughts after that.

Right now, all I want is a shower and then to curl up in that huge bed with Greer in my arms. Simple man, simple needs.

"Shower and sleep?"

She covers her yawn with a hand and nods. "Yes, please. As long as I don't fall asleep standing right here."

"You go first. I'm going to check out the rest of the

house and make sure it's locked up."

By the time I return to the bedroom, Greer is already out of the shower and sound asleep in bed. Naked.

My shower's going to take a little longer . . . because now I've got a raging hard-on to take care of.

CHAPTER
EIGHTEEN

Greer

Waking up with a man wrapped around me and the sound of waves crashing against the shore is decadent. I blink my eyes open to be almost blinded by the bright light streaming in through the windows, sparkling off the surface of the water outside.

Heaven. I've died and woken up in heaven.

I squint against the brightness and arch into the hard, muscled body behind me. Holy shit, his morning wood is more like a morning tree trunk. I lick my lips, intrigued at the thought of waking him up with his cock in my mouth.

Paradise, I love you.

I've wondered for years what it would be like to fall asleep with Cav and wake up next to him, and while I don't remember what it was like to fall asleep next to him, I can certainly make waking up a memorable experience for both of us.

Very carefully, I lift his arm from where it's curled under my boobs and slide out from beneath it. I wait silently, hoping he stays asleep. Soundlessly, he rolls to his back and throws an arm up over his head.

Perfect.

Carefully, I slide the sheet down his torso, revealing the ridges of his abs and the dark trail of hair leading to my prize. I've never wanted a dick in my mouth this badly before. It's an odd compulsion, but I can't ignore the power I feel at the thought of having this powerful man at my mercy.

One more tug of the sheet reveals his thick, hard cock. *Perfection.* Squeezing my thighs together to stem the growing ache, I lower my mouth to trail my lips from the head and down the vein that runs along the shaft. Cav's hips shift when I reach his balls, which are already drawing tighter from the single caress.

I did mention my mad dick-sucking skills, right? Because that's one talent I mastered in my *I'm a virgin, but we can still get each other off* days.

Thank God for misguided teenage ideals.

I glance up at Cav and find his hooded hazel eyes on me. A flash of insecurity hits me. What if my skills are only impressive to guys with a million times less experience than Cav? I wasn't the only girl to lust after him while I was in law school, and I've seen plenty of pictures on gossip sites and magazines with gorgeous actresses that I can in no way compare to.

Cav reaches down and slides his hand into the hair

that's falling over my shoulder. "Waking up with you makes it a hell of a good morning, baby girl. But waking up with your lips on my cock? Fucking incredible."

My momentary hesitation evaporates with his husky words, and I wrap my hand around his shaft and angle it toward my mouth. "Then you're going to love this, Hollywood."

I take him as deep as I can on the first pass and don't stop trying until he's touching the back of my throat. Cav's groans urge me on as I work him deeper and faster. Heat builds between my legs as his fingers tangle in my hair on both sides and his hips lift toward my face. Pulling back for a breath, I cup his balls with one hand and jack the shaft with the other. I'm pretty sure this is the universal girl move for blowjob break.

"Fuck, baby. You're gonna take it from me, aren't you?" Cav growls, his stare boring into me.

I bite my lip and nod, still jacking his cock with one hand. With each movement, his thick thighs flex and tighten.

"I'm going to swallow every drop," I tell him slowly.

"Fuck yes, you are. Every drop is going down that pretty throat of yours. You're going to have my cum in your mouth, your pussy, and your ass before we leave this place."

Heat floods my center. Who knew dirty talk flipped the switch so damn quickly? And him talking about filling my ass . . . it scares me, but intrigues me just as much.

Pushing that thought away for another time, I lower my head to finish the job I started and blow Cav's mind.

Minutes later, his groans are growing louder and his hips are bucking faster into my mouth. I'm letting him fuck my face while I suck and stroke and lick. And it's *phenomenal*. A complete power trip.

"Baby," he says, low and urgent, and I know he's about to come.

His hand grips my hair and holds my head in place as he fucks my mouth and explodes.

Just like he ordered, I swallow every drop.

CHAPTER
NINETEEN

Cav

I'm so fucked. She's it. The one. And I have no right to keep her until I tell her the truth.

Greer wipes a hand delicately across her face like she didn't just give me the blow job to end all blow jobs and swallowed every drop of my cum. What's the saying? A lady in the streets and a whore between the sheets? Greer's no one's whore, but fuck if she isn't a dirty girl. And I love it. Every single fucking bit of it.

After we find the walk-in closet stocked with clothes that surprisingly fit us both, we venture into the dining room to see platters of French toast sprinkled with powdered sugar, as well as eggs, bacon, beans, tortillas, and a spread of fresh-cut fruit. A darker-skinned woman who I assume is Rea sets out syrup.

"This looks amazing." Greer's words are followed by

the growl of her stomach.

I pull her against my side. "We need to get some food into you, baby."

When she smiles up at me, I lean down and press a kiss to her lips.

Rea watches this exchange and waits until we're seated to introduce herself formally.

Greer chats with her as we serve ourselves breakfast. Rea leaves us with fresh, rich coffee and we dive into the food.

Rolling waves crash against the small beach out front, and the infinity pool pours over the side of the tiled deck. This place is epic, and I want to keep Greer locked away here forever. Away from the bullshit waiting for me on both coasts.

I load scrambled eggs, bacon, and beans into a fresh tortilla as Greer sips orange juice and piles French toast, bacon, eggs, and pineapple on her plate.

"I always imagined my honeymoon would be like this." Her words are quiet, but when they land between us like a bomb in the silence of the room, Greer's expression shutters immediately. "I mean, you know, when I was thinking about those things. A million years ago. Never mind. Please rewind the last fifteen seconds and let's start over."

I remember the thoughts I had last night. I was right about where she stands.

Trying to lighten the mood, I say, "I would expect you to have good taste. This place is pretty fucking awesome."

"I'm surprised you're impressed by it," she says,

crunching on a piece of crispy bacon.

Her comment catches me off guard. "You're surprised *I'm* impressed? I'm surprised you are. I was thinking this probably isn't up to your normal Karas luxury standards."

Greer drops the bacon on her plate and wipes her fingertips on the napkin in her lap. "Because you think I'm a spoiled brat? I'm not. At least, not like you think. The trips I took out of New York were few and far between. My uncle didn't like to travel and never took us with him when he did, and when Creighton started traveling a lot, he didn't exactly want his little sister tagging along. I've done Christmas in the Virgin Islands once or twice, and taken spring break trips with friends in college to a couple of resorts Creighton's companies own, but not much more than that. You've probably seen more fancy stuff living in LA than I have."

Her answer surprises me, and she must read it in my expression. "What? You think just because I am who I am that my life has been one jet-setting experience after another? The list of places I want to visit is long. Really long. And you know what? Maybe I don't even want to live in New York forever. Maybe I want to see what it's like to live somewhere other than the East Coast."

I lower my breakfast burrito to my plate and reach for the fresh-squeezed orange juice before me and take a drink.

"Then why don't you?" My question is simple, but the answer matters. "You've got the means to live any kind of life you want, so what's stopping you?"

Greer reaches for her bacon and shoves the remaining

piece in her mouth. "It's not that easy. I can't just pick up and go wherever I want, whenever I want. I need to earn the right to do that, and I'm not anywhere close."

And that right there is one of the reasons I'm so drawn to Greer. She's not a flighty heiress content to live on her trust fund. She's driven, and may be the one person who can relate to my need to prove myself.

"I understand that. Then, I guess, cheers to earning the right to do whatever the fuck you want." I lift my glass and wait for her to pick hers up before I clink the rims together.

Midway through her French toast, Greer tosses an unexpected question at me. "Do you feel like you're tied down in Hollywood now?"

"What do you mean?"

"Like, do they own your life and your future?"

I take a bite of my breakfast burrito and consider her question as I chew. "No one owns me or my future. It's what I make of it, and I refuse to let anyone dictate to me. I've gotten myself to this level, and I'm just stashing cash so I can walk away whenever I want."

Greer forks up another chunk of French toast as she watches me. "Fair enough. I can respect that. That's a lot of the reason I wanted to earn my own salary rather than live off interest and dividends from my trust fund and the Karas companies. There's always strings attached to everything."

She lowers her fork and spins it between her thumb and finger. "But then again, I guess it doesn't matter if I live off the money or not. Creighton's still dictating my behavior when it really impacts the company. Some days I wish I could just change my last name. I mean, I love my brother and I'm crazy proud of what he's accomplished, but living under a microscope isn't so much fun." She stops playing with the fork and lowers it to the plate. "First-world problems, I know."

I consider her words for only a moment before landing on a solution. "You can be whoever you want to be here, Greer. No one knows who we are or why we're here, so let's have fun with it. So just decide—who do you want to be?"

Greer's dark eyes light up with the possibility. "Well, damn. I've never thought about that. I need some time."

CHAPTER
TWENTY

Greer

Cav doesn't realize what he's done by setting loose my imagination. Has anything ever been quite so seductive as that one question—*who do you want to be?* As if I can just choose whoever that is and it can happen. But maybe here, on this island where no one knows who we are, I truly can.

Rea comes in and cleans up breakfast as I make my way back to the bedroom. The cool tile is refreshing under my feet as the heat from the sun is already warming the house.

Yes, paradise, I really do love you.

In my borrowed shorts and tank, I investigate my swimsuit options in the walk-in closet. The lure of the infinity pool is strong, and it seems like the perfect place to relax and decide exactly what or who I want to be while

I'm here.

In my head, one answer is already bubbling to the surface and mocking me. Do I have the guts to say it aloud?

If this is all pretend and temporary, why not play the part? I'm not going to get to keep Cav Westman, but maybe I can pretend for a little while.

It's going to take a hell of a lot of liquor to find the lady balls to say what I'm thinking.

Slipping into a neon-pink suit that's only a little too small in the tits and ass areas, because apparently whoever owns this place has curves that are less generous than mine, I grab some sunscreen out of the bathroom cabinet and wander out toward the pool.

I pause and admire the sight before me when I see Cav has already stripped off his shirt. His board shorts are riding low, exposing the vee cut at his hips. Those lines really do make girls stupid. I had his dick in my mouth just before breakfast, and now I want to sink to my knees and lick those indents and then those abs . . .

The critics who say he's been photoshopped? Liars. All liars. Because damn, if the ladies of the world could see what I'm seeing right now, I'm pretty sure they'd all want to hunt me down and take my place. Headlines would read GREER KARAS SHANKS RIVAL WOMEN IN CAT FIGHT OVER HOLLYWOOD SEX GOD.

God, wouldn't Creighton be pissed then?

"You need someone to volunteer to help you with that sunscreen, baby?"

Silencing the giggle bubbling up my throat before it can come out, I nod. "Yes, but I do think it's time to ditch the *whitest white girl on the beach* look."

"You're not the whitest white girl on the beach." He tilts his head to the side, studying me. "But you do have a touch of that *New York city dweller* look to you."

"I'm a ghost because I stay indoors all the time. As opposed to you, sun-bronzed god over there, living it up in Cali and looking fine."

One eyebrow rises at my blurted words. "The only place you need to think I'm a god is in the bedroom, baby."

He looks from one side of the secluded deck to the other. The neighbors' houses are at least fifty yards away on each side and nearly impossible to see through the thick forest of coconut and palm trees.

"Lose the top. There's no reason for unnecessary tan lines."

I don't have major body-confidence issues, and it's not like he hasn't already seen me naked, but something about stripping outside seems so . . . naughty.

Cav's expression takes on a serious cast I haven't seen before. "Did you think there was something optional about that? It was an order, Greer. I want to see those pretty tits in the sunlight."

I blink twice, not sure I heard him correctly. "Wha— what did you say?"

Cav steps toward me, solidly masculine and sexy as hell. But what's with the bossiness? The sensation of the cool granite on my cheek as I laid over the countertop in my kitchen resurfaces in my memory. He was plenty bossy then. But I thought maybe it was something that only extended to sex.

He stops in front of me and studies me. "You heard me, baby girl. I've decided who I want you to be while we're here. Now you just have to tell me you want it too."

"Want what?" My confusion comes out in my tone. "I thought this was supposed to be my decision. Whoever I wanted to be?"

"You can still be whoever you want, but this is my layer of . . . extra, that I want."

Heat flushes my skin and dampness gathers between my legs. Is this really turning me on?

Cav lifts a hand and instead of reaching for the bikini strap, he skims the back of his hand over my very hard nipple that's obviously poking against the top.

So that's a yes from my body.

"You want it too, Greer. You want me to tell you what I want from you and make you give it to me." He steps closer, continuing to speak before I can form words to respond. "You've been waiting for someone to come into your life and treat you like the dirty girl we both know you are, haven't you?"

Skip *damp*—my bikini bottoms are now soaked, and I haven't dipped a toe in the pool. How did he get inside my head and pull out my most forbidden thoughts? I think I instinctively hadn't trusted Tristan enough to give him that kind of power, but with Cav I have a completely different gut-level feeling.

I swallow, trying to come up with a response. My internal struggle must be emblazoned on my reddening cheeks, because Cav lifts a hand to my chin and tilts it up to face him. "All you have to do is say *yes*, Greer."

"Where . . . where did this come from? What makes you think I want this?"

A lazy smile spreads over his face. "I know you better than you think. Do you remember the first time I told you to kiss me? You wanted me to take the lead. Make the decision. Tell you what to do. It hasn't changed a bit." He releases my chin and trails the back of his fingers across my cheek before burying his hand in my hair. "Tell me what you did when I told you to kiss me. Do you remember how sweet you were? How willing to please?"

The memory comes back as if on his command . . .

Cav insisted we share a taxi home from the bar, and the driver stopped at my place near campus. He got out of the car first, telling the cabbie to wait, and walked me to the front door. When I thanked him for the drinks and the ride, he shook his head.

"I'm walking you to your apartment door. I'm not some punk kid who's going to leave a girl on the sidewalk." He looked down at the ink covering his arm, exposed without a jacket. "I may look like a thug, but I've got a few manners in me."

I had just enough liquor to speak my mind without a filter. "You don't look like a thug. You look . . . sexy as hell." Once the words were out, I reconsidered my honesty. "Shit, I shouldn't say things like that. You—"

"Like knowing the girl I think is hot as fuck also thinks I'm sexy as hell." His grin was wicked, and my body—aka my nipples—took notice and stiffened against my bra. "You're so damn innocent, but I still want a taste, Greer. Lead the way."

What did that even mean, he still wanted a taste? And I wasn't that innocent. I wasn't a virgin or anything. I just didn't fuck on the first date. My thoughts were coming in jumbled riots as I led him to the elevator and up the hall-way.

I stopped in front of my door. "This one."

Cav held out his hand. "Keys."

"You're bossy."

A crooked smirk twitched the corner of his mouth. "You have no idea, baby girl. You have no idea."

I didn't know what that meant, but I handed over the keys and watched him unlock my door. I stepped over the threshold, but Cav wrapped a hand around my arm to stop me.

"You're gonna kiss me first, and then you can go to bed."

"I'm gonna kiss you?" Surprise filtered into my tone at his bossy statement.

"Like you've been waiting weeks to do it."

Which was the God's honest truth.

I stared up into his changing hazel eyes. In this light, they were bluish-gray. How was I supposed to just . . . kiss him?

"Well, this is awkward," I murmured.

"Doesn't have to be awkward at all. All you gotta do is exactly what I say."

He walked me through it, one step at a time, exactly

how he wanted me to kiss him. Both hands on his chest, pressing up on the toes of my boots until our lips met, and then he took control.

I knew it at that moment—Cav Westman's dominant streak ran hot.

"I remember," I whisper. "But—"

"But nothing. I want you to let go, Greer. Let me take the wheel for a while. I swear you'll enjoy the hell out of it."

I know what my answer is, but instead of speaking the words, I reach for the ties on my bikini top and tug them free. The hot-pink material slides away and I drop it on the lounge chair beside me.

Cav's eyes heat with lust. He reaches up and cups my breast, leaning down to whisper against my lips, "Fucking beautiful. And all mine."

A thought strikes me. "What about Rea and Juan? I don't—"

"I told her we'd take care of making our own lunch. Neither of them will be coming in the house until tonight." His thumb brushes across my nipple, taunting it into a harder peak. "You think I want to share you with anyone? This is all for me and no one else."

The possessiveness in his words unknots the ball of anxiety twisting in my belly. Maybe I can ask for what I want just like he's demanded exactly what he wants from me.

Soon. Later. *Once I've had time to properly construct the words and analyze all of the responses he could give me.* Why is it I can be completely impulsive with some things and then absolutely analytical in others?

Oh, that's right. Alcohol. Speaking of which . . .

Cav reads my mind. "Let's get this sexy skin protected from the sun, and then I'm going to make us a round of drinks. I'm gonna eat your pussy while you drink it."

"Say what now?" I squeak.

"Your pussy. You woke me with your mouth on my cock, and I'm feeling deprived. Call it my midmorning snack." His wicked grin ensures my stiff nipples aren't disappearing anytime soon. "Now, lay down on the lounge chair so I can take care of you."

I follow his directive, lying first on my stomach and letting him cover me with sunscreen. Cav's wide hands take only seconds to cover the expanse of my shoulders, back, and legs.

When I roll over and try to grab the sunscreen from him, he holds it out of reach. "Really, Greer, you think I'm going to pass up any opportunity to get my hands all over you?"

"Do I get to return the favor?"

A smile curves lazily along his lips, and the urge to kiss him beats strongly within me.

"Absolutely."

I smother my moans as Cav takes his time covering every inch of my skin with sunscreen. Kneading my breasts and rolling my nipples is unnecessary, but a completely welcome addition. By the time he's finished, I'm bucking my hips against the knee pressing between my legs.

"You tempt the hell out of me, baby girl." He shifts his knee, replacing it with his palm between my legs, pressing the heel of his hand into my clit. The focused pressure is exactly what I need. I'm shameless, grinding myself against him, my orgasm just out of reach.

"You wanna come?"

"Yes," I whisper, rocking against him.

"Are you gonna come hard?" He rolls my nipple between his fingers, and spears of pleasure lance through me. I'm so close.

"Yes," I promise.

"Then come for me, baby. I wanna hear you moan my name. And then I want your pussy in my face."

His dirty words unleash another layer of sensation, and I'm teetering on the edge.

"And while I eat this sweet cunt, I'm going to play with that tight little asshole, stretch it out so you're ready to take me. I will have every part of you, baby. Mouth, pussy, ass. Might fuck these gorgeous tits and make you swallow my cum again."

"Ahhhh, Cav." I moan his name as my climax breaks free, my entire body shaking against his hold. It rolls through me, wave after shimmering wave until I finally still.

Cav lowers his head and tugs my bottom lip between his teeth. "I fucking love watching you come. Every day, as many times a day as you can stand it."

His hand skims down my body and finds the ties on

the sides of my bikini bottoms. With a tug, one side falls free.

"Now it's my turn."

CHAPTER
TWENTY-ONE

Cav

I'll never get enough of Greer. I know it as she's smothering her screams with a hand, my mouth on her clit and one finger teasing her ass. Fuck, she's perfect. She's everything I wanted her to be three years ago, and the loss of time haunts me, even though I know I had no choice.

After she collapses, spent, on the lounge, I rise and adjust my cock in my board shorts. Not fucking her right now takes an inordinate amount of restraint, but this is about her, not me. I want her thinking about all the dirty promises I just made her. I want her thinking of me as much as I'm thinking of her. It seems nearly impossible because she's infiltrated my thoughts on every level.

"You look like you could use a drink, baby," I say as I watch some of the pink flush fade from her cheekbones.

Greer nods. "Please. Anything. You want some help?"

"Not necessary, but if you want, I'll take your company."

She reaches for her bikini top with a smile, but I'm quicker.

"No top. I want your tits out for me."

The flush of her cheeks is back in an instant. Greer is strong-willed, opinionated, and not someone most people would suspect of having a submissive streak. I saw it early on, and even though part of me thought it was simply wishful thinking, a little time proved me right.

Regardless, each time I give her an order when we're not fucking, it unbridles a struggle within her. I don't think it's that she wants to say no, she just fights against her independence every time she says yes. It's a beautiful struggle and one I'm incredibly grateful to receive the benefits of. She always thinks about telling me to go fuck myself—I can see it. But it turns her on even more to obey. I want that from her because every time she bends to my will, her addiction to me grows.

When she stands, slipping into her bikini bottoms but leaving the top behind, I know which part of her mind won the battle. Grabbing her by the hand, I pull her into the house toward the kitchen.

Fresh pineapple is wrapped up in the fridge from breakfast, along with pitchers of fresh pineapple juice and orange juice. I grab the pineapple and direct Greer to the well-stocked liquor cabinet. Three kinds of rum splash into the blender along with the pineapple, juice, and ice. As our drinks blend, Greer stands beside me with my arm wrapped around her shoulders.

Her voice is quiet when she speaks. "You asked who I wanted to be . . ."

I glance down at her face to see her worrying her bottom lip between her teeth.

"And?" I wonder where she's going with this because her posture is rigid. I only have to wait a few more beats before she speaks again.

"What if I want this?"

"What do you mean?"

"This easiness. Like those years haven't passed without us being together, and this is just our regular vacation. No ad, no press hounding us, no brother sending us away. Just . . . us. Being us." She covers her face with her palm. "God, now I'm just babbling. Never mind. Forget I said anything."

Warmth gathers in my chest, something I didn't actually know was possible. I want what she wants. No guilt, no lies, no secrets. Just us together, and even better, pretending this is our normal. Our life. Fuck, I'd kill for that to be the truth.

"I'm not forgetting shit, because I want that too. You can have whatever you want, Greer. And if that's what you want, then it's all yours."

"You don't think that makes me sound crazy?" She seems shy and unsure, not at all like the confident Greer I see most often.

I squeeze her against my side. "I think it makes you sweet and fucking perfect."

I turn off the blender and pour our drinks into two glasses. Handing one to Greer, I raise mine in a toast.

"To us."

Her smile flashes brilliantly now as she clinks her glass against mine. "To us."

CHAPTER
TWENTY-TWO

Greer

Sometimes leaps of faith are rewarded with the best possible outcome you can imagine. Apparently being brave and telling someone what you want can actually be a good thing.

As I stand in the kitchen helping Cav make us lunch, my skin warm from the Belizean sun, I feel like I've gotten my reward. I finish chopping up veggies to toss in the salad, and he pours the shrimp he sautéed into a bowl. Let's just say if I hadn't already staked my pretend claim on this man, watching him cook would have the words tumbling out of my mouth.

"Another round of drinks?" he asks.

I'm already halfway to day drunk, so I'm more than on board. "Definitely."

With efficient movements, he blends another pitcher,

and I carry the salad and heaping bowl of shrimp out to the table on the patio. The Caribbean Sea is calm today, but that's largely due to the barrier reef that's not far offshore.

I can't help but send a mental thanks to my brother for setting this up. I wish I knew whose house we were crashing, but I can't get details right now. I checked my phone earlier, hoping the No Service label would have magically changed. It didn't. No Wi-Fi connection either. I'm taking that as a blessing in disguise. Being completely cut off from the world is somehow liberating. It's just Cav and me, on our own.

He joins me with the drinks, and we pile our plates full.

"How about we go out and explore the village for dinner?"

Taking a sip of the tropical drink—*ah, heaven*—I nod. "I like that idea."

"I like the idea of being able to go out in public with you and not having to worry that either of us will be recognized. We owe your brother a thank-you, although I'm not sure he's going to want to hear it from me."

I reach for my fork and spear into a shrimp. "He's probably already congratulating himself on this being an amazing idea because it gets me out of the way so effectively. Creighton doesn't miss any chances to validate his genius."

"You get along with him, though, don't you?"

Chewing my mouthful of lunch, I pause before I answer. "Absolutely. He's the most important person in my life. My aunt flakes out a lot, but I blame that on my uncle."

Cav pauses as he reaches for his drink. "What's your uncle's story?"

I shake my head. "It's a long one. Besides . . . he, um, took a leave of absence to go to rehab."

I know my statement is going to raise more than one question, but it's unavoidable. I can't exactly tell Cav that the mob made my uncle disappear as a favor to my brother, and no one really misses him much. Not exactly casual lunch conversation. Besides, the family mob connection isn't one that I'm even allowed to speak about. It's been kept under wraps for over thirty years, and no one is going to bring it to light now.

The rehab story was the best solution for my uncle's absence. Everyone knows he was a functional alcoholic, and it was only a matter of time before he lost the "functional" piece. It's a measure of exactly how little he was liked that no one questioned it or asked for an address so they could visit.

"That must be hard on your family," Cav says, his tone sympathetic. "I remember you saying your parents had passed when you were a baby?"

"Good memory. I didn't know either of them. I was mostly raised by nannies, and occasionally my aunt. Creighton came home as much as he could, but he was away at school. I don't think he ever would have come home, though, had it not been for me."

"That explains the headlines a while back when things went to shit between your uncle and your brother."

I ate another shrimp before replying. "No love lost

there, that's for sure." *Understatement of the century.* "But I'd rather talk about you. My life is boring, and you've heard most of it already."

"It's not boring. I want to know you, Greer. This isn't just us fucking."

My heart clenches when he says exactly what I want to hear. But how much of it can I trust? He pulled his own disappearing act before, and I still haven't worked up the guts to demand the full explanation. But I will. I need to know, need to understand, before I can trust him again. And I want to trust him so badly, I can taste it.

I let the questions slide for now, not wanting to shatter the idyllic day by getting an answer I don't want to hear. Am I burying my head in the sand? Absolutely. But for now, just for a little while, I want to pretend that everything's perfect.

After we clear our plates, I settle onto a raft, and Cav finds the stereo system and cranks up some reggae. *This* is paradise.

But why do I feel like it's the calm before the storm?

CHAPTER
TWENTY-THREE

Greer

I'm in love with a shower. Well, not the shower itself, but how Cav lifts me so effortlessly and plunges his cock inside me over and over while the water beats down on us both. Digging my nails into his shoulders, I struggle to hold on to him and the words that want to fall from my lips.

That I need him. I'm dying for him. I need his cock and the orgasm he's been teasing me with for the last ten minutes.

"Please," I say on a moan. "Please."

"You're not gonna come until I say you can come."

Cav's dominance is revving my senses in unexpected ways. I'm more daring, sassier, pushing against his boundaries and the limits of pleasure. Every sensation is enhanced a dozen times over. The spray of the water, the thrust of his cock, and the pressure on my clit. I want to come like I've never wanted to come before, and it's all because he's told me I can't.

"Please," I beg again. "I need—"

"You need me fucking you the way I want to give it to you." He pulls me down on his shaft and I grind my clit against his lower abs, determined to steal this orgasm whether he wants me to or not. My brain is in pursuit of pleasure and won't be denied.

It's rolling through me, but I hold back the scream. Like a thief, I latch on to the climax and let it crash down on me. My inner muscles convulse on his cock and Cav freezes, pinning me to the wall with his intense stare and muscles gone rigid.

"You naughty little girl. I told you not to come, but you didn't listen."

My body is buzzing with the orgasm, and there's not a damn thing he can do about it. He can't take it back.

Feeling bold, I wink. "What are you going to do about it, Hollywood?"

Heat burns in his gaze. "Teach you a lesson."

My pussy clamps down on his cock instinctively. Yep, my body likes the idea of Cav teaching me a lesson just a little too much. He doesn't miss the squeeze either.

Shaking his head slowly, Cav tightens his grip on my ass with both hands. "We're done with this shower." He turns to the open section in the tile enclosure and lifts me off his cock before lowering me to my feet. His eyes never leave mine as he shuts off the water, grabs a towel, and wraps it around me.

A shred of apprehension forms in my stomach. *What is he going to do?*

Cav can read me too easily, because his lips form a forbidding smile. He doesn't reach for his own towel, just grasps my upper arms and rubs them through the terry-cloth, drying me wordlessly, his cock still hard and ready.

The shred of apprehension grows.

"What is this lesson?" I ask, my voice more hesitant than I've ever heard it.

Cav doesn't reply, just continues drying me off. When I'm sufficiently dry, he uses the same towel on himself. Once he's finished, he loops it over the rack and returns his attention to me.

"You're going to go into the bedroom, bend over the bed, and wait for me. Arms out. Palms flat. Ass up."

My nipples harden into tight peaks at his command. Arousal swirls with the apprehension.

"What are you going to—"

"Go."

I still at the authority in his tone. He's not fucking around, and part of me loves it. Namely, my pussy, which is already growing wetter again by the second.

Teeth digging into my lower lip, I hesitate another few seconds, the challenge hanging between us, before I turn and take measured steps into the bedroom. The white coverlet is laid out innocently before me. Whatever Cav is going to do with me is going to be anything but innocent.

The four-poster bed with its gauzy white hangings blowing in the breeze that seemed so romantic only an hour before now holds a million other possibilities.

Will he tie me down? Make me wait for his command? Take me however he wants?

Each possibility is more tantalizing than the last. If someone asked me whether I had a submissive streak, I would have confidently said absolutely not, but faced with Cav's dominance, my will is bending and my answer is changing.

It's him. He's the one who brings this out in me. And it's just a game. Right?

"You're not following directions."

His deep voice comes from behind me, raising chill bumps along my skin. Without looking back, I fold my body over the high mattress, which is at the perfect height for me to stand, my ass in the air as he commanded.

"Determined to add to your punishment, baby girl? Because I'll gladly oblige."

Shivers whisper across my skin as his footsteps come nearer. His fingertips glide along the curve of my ass from hip to hip and then back again.

"I bet you didn't realize how fascinated I was with your ass three years ago. I used to fantasize about having you at my mercy, tied down, taking you every way I wanted." His fingers lightly glide between my cheeks. "And this ass played a big role in those fantasies."

His touch disappears until I feel a rush of air and then a sharp *slap* landing on my right cheek. I jump at the stinging contact, as if trying to move out of the strike zone.

Cav's other hand presses against the small of my back, stilling my movements. "There's no escaping your punishment, baby girl. You agreed to play my game, and you're going to take every smack you deserve for stealing that orgasm." He lowers to speak closer to my ear. "And you're gonna fucking love it."

Again, shivers race over my skin as his fingers trail lazily across me, increased sensitivity following his every move.

He pulls away and I tense, my muscles anticipating the strikes to come. And they *come*. Over and over, Cav's wide palm connects with my ass, leaving a shimmer of heat behind with every slap.

"Fuck, baby. I love seeing your ass turn red from my hand. You're such a good girl. Not moving, waiting for more."

When he stops after a final smack, he cups and kneads my burning cheeks with both hands. He spreads them wide and I squirm against the covers, not sure what he's doing next. But he releases me and steps away.

Face turned sideways on the coverlet, I watch as he leaves the bedroom and returns a moment later with a bottle of coconut oil from the kitchen. My first thought is a massage, but my stinging ass contradicts me.

Oh. Hell.

My last bastion of virginity may be in jeopardy.

"What are you going to do with—"

The wicked gleam in his hazel eyes cuts me off. "Whatever I want."

Heart hammering in my chest, I lose sight of Cav as he steps behind me.

"Seriously, I've never—"

"Had a cock in this sweet little ass? Haven't been properly corrupted and fucked?"

I have to be leaving a mark on the bed, because I don't think I've ever been this wet in my life. And I also don't have an answer.

"Don't worry, baby girl. I'm gonna take good care of you."

Anticipation. Apprehension. Curiosity mixed with a twinge of good old-fashioned fear. It's all there, running through my veins and kicking my heart rate up another notch. I don't have to wait long to feel the warm dribble of oil at the top of my crack. Here, in the heat, it doesn't solidify the way it does at home . . . making it perfect for Cav's purpose.

His fingers follow the trail of warm oil, sliding down between my cheeks until he hits the pucker of my ass.

Oh my God. Oh my God. Oh my God. My breathing picks up speed along with the hammering of my heart.

This is happening.

"This ass is mine," Cav drawls as he presses against it. But before he penetrates, his other hand slides under my hips and strokes my clit. "And so is this pussy. Tight little cunt that comes when it's not supposed to." In a simultaneous motion, he pinches my clit between the sides of two fingers and presses into my ass with his fingertip.

Moisture drenches his hand as I push against him, seeking the pressure on my clit and sneaking away from the pressure against my ass.

It doesn't work. The nerve endings flare to life as his finger slides further inside.

The pressure gives way to dark, spine-arching pleasure. Suddenly I'm pressing back against one hand and rocking forward for the friction on my clit.

"Your ass is going to strangle my cock, and it's going to be fucking perfect."

A second fingertip teases the edge, but doesn't press inside. Not yet. His fingers begin to move, all of them. The friction on my clit climbs and climbs until my entire body is vibrating on the edge of an orgasm.

Do I come? Do I wait? What do I do?

In and out, his other finger slides into the forbidden until a second one joins it, stretching me further. Once again, nerve endings flare to life, setting off alarms in my head that my climax is close.

"I'm going to—"

"Not yet, baby."

His hands leave my body.

"Wait—"

"Fuck. I know I can't have your ass yet, but goddammit, I want it."

The head of Cav's cock fits against my entrance and he thrusts, filling my pussy before I'm prepared. He doesn't slow. Doesn't wait, just pounds into me. I claw at the coverlet, trying to hold off my orgasm until he tells me I can come. It's growing bigger and bolder and unstoppable.

"You want to know what it's like to have your pussy and your ass filled at the same time, baby?"

My mind is still processing his words when something presses against my asshole and slides inside.

Holy. Hell.

He fucks me in alternating strokes, thumb and cock,

dragging whimpers and moans of pleasure from my lips. I'm losing my grip. I can't hold off.

"Now. Come now," Cav orders.

I let go and my climax barrels through my body, starting at my center and crashing outward.

Cav doesn't slow, doesn't pause.

"Fuuuck." He pulls out, and hot jets of cum spray on my ass.

Neither of us moves for several heartbeats until Cav drags his fingers through the semen cooling on my skin.

"You're going to need another shower, baby girl."

A giggle escapes my lips because that's the truth.

"And you're one step closer to taking my cock." His voice quiets when he adds, "I love knowing that I'll be the first. It's fucking primal. Just like the way I marked you tonight."

That's why he pulled out? To mark me?

Another tremor spirals down my spine. Who knew he would be so possessive?

He moves away once more, and I hear water running for a couple of minutes before he returns with a washcloth to clean me up. When I rise, Cav pulls me into his arms and presses a kiss to the top of my head.

"You took your punishment well."

My cheeks flame red. Now I know I can handle doing it, but talking about it after? That's pushing a completely new limit.

"You're going to disobey again, aren't you? Because you liked what I did to you."

I did like it. I can't deny it. But the words won't come.

Admitting I loved this and want more of it seems beyond my abilities right now.

And then I recall one liberating fact. *I can be whoever I want while we're here. I can take what I want and what I need.*

I press a hand to Cav's muscled chest. "The chances of me disobeying your orders again are a high probability."

His wicked grin validates my confession. He wants me to want this as badly as I do.

Another unexpected and quick *smack* lands on my ass, and I jump.

"Into the shower with you. And then get ready to explore the village. We're leaving the compound."

CHAPTER
TWENTY-FOUR

Cav

Fuck. I'm in deep. I knew it before, but every moment I spend with Greer highlights the fact even more brightly. I shouldn't have come back, but I couldn't stay away. How can one person draw you in so much?

Sitting across the table from her at a hole in the wall on the beach has me thinking about how simple and fucking complicated life can be at the same time. Here on this tiny island, no one knows who we are, and part of me wants to live like this forever. Fuck, if I'd brought my ropes, I'd tie her to that bed and we'd never leave. I'd feed her from my hand and keep her coming too much to complain.

Reality won't take long to intrude, but I'm doing the best I can to keep it away. I disabled the router and flipped a setting on Greer's phone so she can't get cell service.

I know what kind of phone call will come, and I'm not

ready. So I've taken steps to keep us isolated longer. My own phone is turned off because I have no doubt it would be blowing up.

If only I'd already done more movies and banked an extra few million, I'd be tempted to buy one of the deserted cays not far from here and keep her with me there forever.

But with a brother as powerful as Creighton Karas, I could only keep Greer hidden so long from the world.

She's sipping a Panty Ripper and smiling at me mischievously. I want her to myself, and her asking to pretend like this is real, as if I never walked out on her, is exactly what I want to hear.

"What?" I take a drink of my Long Island iced tea as she bites her lip.

Greer is on drink number three, so it's no surprise that she's giggling when she says, "I'd let you rip my panties—if I were wearing any."

She winks at me, poorly, with both eyes closed, and that's when I get a clue that Greer and Belizean rum aren't to be mixed too heavily.

I drop my gaze instantly to the sandy floor beneath our feet and lock onto the short purple skirt she raided from the walk-in closet.

"You're a naughty little thing, aren't you?"

"It's you and the rum. And because I wasn't about to wear someone else's panties." She shivers in disgust.

"Fair enough." I'm commando under my shorts, so I get it. "So that means no panties the entire time we're here. I think I'm going to have fun with that little piece of information."

She leans in closer. "Oh yeah?"

I nod slowly, ideas already springing to life in my head—along with my cock in my shorts. I need to turn this conversation to another topic.

"I think it's time we get some food in you, baby."

I lift my chin in the direction of the waitress lounging behind the bar, playing on her phone. She's working on island time, but she must get the sense she's going to get a decent tip because she tears off the ticket and crosses to the table more quickly than I've seen her move yet this afternoon.

I pay the tab and pull Greer from her seat.

"I'm not done with my Panty Ripper yet," she protests.

"Food, woman. Or you'll be passing out on me before we get home."

"I'm not that drunk. Seriously. I can handle a few rum punch drinks."

I watch her, expecting her to sway on her feet, but she's steady. "Maybe you can."

"You don't know everything about me, Hollywood. I've got a few secrets." Her sassy smile is followed by the press of her finger to my chest.

I wish she were the only one with secrets. And fuck, I want to know what her secrets are. I want to know everything.

"Is that right?"

She nods. "Damn right. A few more drinks and you can get me to spill them all."

That makes one of us.

"So, what are you feeding me?"

I lead her out to the street and laugh. "Either lobster, conch, shrimp, or snapper."

Every menu on this island is practically the same from what I can tell as we cruise down the rutted sand street in our golf cart, slowing for the speed bumps, which are nothing more than thick ropes lying across the road. *Whatever gets the job done.*

I spy one restaurant that looks like it has been recently remodeled. The benches are covered in mismatched pillows, and fans blow from every angle.

The chalkboard proclaims they have fresh conch ceviche, which isn't a surprise, but I think Greer will be comfortable eating here. If there's such a thing as an upscale Caye Caulker eatery, I think we've found it.

We settle at a table and put in an order for another round of drinks. It's time to get Greer to spill those secrets.

CHAPTER
TWENTY-FIVE

Greer

I sland time isn't a totally new thing for me, but here on this tiny island, it's a little extreme. We've waited twenty minutes for our drinks and the waitress hasn't returned, so Cav makes his way to the bar to see what's up.

What started out as a quiet afternoon in the village has turned into a busy evening. Backpackers staying in the hostels have ventured out with their dreads in tie-dyed head scarves and reggae music blares from the basketball court that sits right on the ocean.

Business is hopping in this little restaurant, but Cav makes a place for himself at the bar. Several women about my age or maybe younger, wearing shorts bordering on daisy dukes and semi-backless tops, take notice as he lifts his chin at the bartender to ask about our drinks and our waitress.

The bartender nods vigorously and turns to grab liquor bottles off the shelf lining the mirrored bar. Like any man at a bar, Cav gets sucked into small talk. My hands are empty and my buzz is wearing off, so I've got nothing to do but watch him—and the women.

A brunette in white shorts and a pale turquoise midriff-baring halter takes a second look at Cav. Not surprising because the man is looking fine as hell in his borrowed cargo shorts and the T-shirt that fits him snugly across the shoulders and chest.

Shit. Did she recognize him? Is our cover blown? Hell, maybe we should have stayed in the compound for dinner.

But that wouldn't have made this little trip feel like we were something real. Then again, maybe this is the reality of a life we'd have. Always hiding behind walls to stay out of the eye of the paparazzi and fans.

From the way she wobbles on her stool, I'm guessing she might be too wasted to place him. His gray baseball cap covers his hair, and his head is turned in profile. *Maybe she's European and won't recognize him?* I'm not sure how big Cav is over there, but I'm desperately clinging to the hope that we're not going to be outed. On an island this small, we really have nowhere else to hide besides the house. Gossip would spread in hours to every resident of this place.

I watch for a few more moments, nervousness twisting a knot into my stomach as she talks and laughs. Her blond friend joins the conversation, practically falling off her bar stool to get closer to him.

The knot in my stomach soon morphs into something

other than nervousness. They're surrounding him, each with a hand on his arm and one offering up her drink to him. Cav waves it away but the brunette insists, nearly impaling him with the straw. He relents and grabs the glass, sips from the side, and nods in approval.

Another minute and a half of watching these women put their hands on him—his biceps, his shoulder, his fucking abs—has me accepting a simple fact. I'm *jealous*.

I don't get jealous. I can't think of a time in the last two years with Tristan that I ever saw him with another woman and wondered *what the fuck is he doing?* But Cav isn't Tristan. Cav is in a league of his own, the kind of league where men have arms that women, like the blonde, want to wrap their hands around.

I turn away, not wanting to see any more because, frankly, I'm disgusted with how I feel. The knot in my stomach sloshes around the Panty Rippers I drank, and suddenly I don't give a shit about the drinks. I want some food, and I want to get out of here so I can analyze what the hell is going wrong with my brain. Jealous? That's not me.

And over Cav, someone I know for a fact has half of the American female population drooling over him? Someone who is only permanent as long as we stay in this little fantasy we've constructed?

Seriously, Greer? Get over it. I don't have any right to be jealous, but my gut reaction doesn't lie. I don't want to see another woman's hands on my man.

My man? Maybe for however long Creighton decides we need to lay low. Because who knows what's going to happen when I get summoned back to New York. I'm not placing any bets on where this is going.

Stop, I order my brain. I've got tonight and a limited number of days with Cav. I'm not going to waste them feeling like a jealous shrew.

As soon as I give myself that mental slap to the face, Cav returns with our drinks.

I opted for the fresh mango margarita, chancing the jump from rum to tequila in my semi-buzzed bravery. Cav has a bottle of Belikin, the beer of Belize, or so all the signs I've seen proclaim. I tell myself I'm not going to say anything about the women at the bar, but the words come out anyway, and I sound just as bitchy as I did in my head.

"Make some new friends?"

Cav frowns as he pulls off the napkin that's wrapped around the neck of the beer bottle and tucked inside the top. "New friends?"

"At the bar? Did they recognize you? Do we need to vacate the premises and prepare for a paparazzi invasion?"

He laughs and takes a swig. I glance over my shoulder to the bar and find the two women watching him drink.

Uh. No, ladies. Not yours.

When Cav sets the beer back on the table between us, he says, "We're good. No worries. They were just being typical barflies."

Who he let paw at him?

"Well, they seemed pretty friendly."

He takes another drink and nods to my margarita. "Aren't you going to try it?"

I reach for the straw paper and toss it away, sucking

back a healthy swig of the thick drink. It's like a mango smoothie that happens to have booze, and it's delicious. The sweetness helps take the edge off the sour feelings in the pit of my stomach.

"Greer, what's wrong?"

Oh, great. Now I'm clearly telegraphing the fact that I've been smacked with the jealous girlfriend stick. *Except I'm not his girlfriend.* So I do what most women would in my position. I lie.

"Nothing. I'm fine." The sharpness of my tone gives me away instantly. *Epic fail, Greer.*

Cav's hazel eyes study me and he shakes his head. "Bullshit." He pitches his voice lower, and it carries a distinct air of authority. "Spill, woman. Something's up."

Do I continue to lie, or do I come clean and get over this ridiculous flare of jealousy?

I suck back another long, deep drink. Liquid courage at its finest. Cav watches me, not missing my actions. I release the straw and trace a pattern into the condensation forming on the glass.

"I guess I'm not used to seeing other women's hands on you in public. You know, outside of a red carpet photo."

Instantly, I wish I used different words because now he knows I've been following his career. If he only knew that he is one of my top guilty Google searches. I haven't been able to stop myself from typing his name into the search bar at least once every other week or so after he first appeared on the big screen.

That first movie poster on the side of a bus almost caused my death when I stepped into oncoming traffic to get a closer look. Watching the face of the man you put out of your mind—because he disappeared without a good-bye or a fuck-you—roll by on a bus while you're pausing at a crosswalk isn't something I recommend.

I made it to my office, my heart pounding and hands shaking, and logged in to my computer and waited for the browser to load. It was a measure of just how flustered I was that I didn't even think to use my phone. Maybe I knew I needed to see the results on a regular-sized monitor.

Sure enough, there he was. The man who is now watching me across the table, trying to gauge my mood based on my body language and words.

"It's not a big deal, Greer. The blonde said I looked like I could be some kind of action hero, so I took a minute to kill their dreams and told them that I was a fertilizer salesman from Tulsa. I couldn't think of anything less interesting than a guy selling shit for a living."

I choke back a laugh, glad I wasn't sucking down my drink in earnest at that moment. "That's your cover story? Fertilizer salesman from Tulsa? Wow."

This time I do reach for my mango deliciousness, giggling as I sip.

Cav shrugs. "It works. Their hands were gone pretty damn quick after that. Shit isn't a sexy business."

"Where did you even get that?"

He lifts his beer to his lips, as if unsure where that random-as-hell answer came from. When he lowers the Belikin to the table, his answer surprises me.

"My dad used that one when I was growing up."

Confusion has me pausing before taking another drink. "Why did your dad lie about what he did?"

Cav twists the bottle in his hands. "He didn't always like to share the whole story. Said it was no one's business."

More confusion and more questions bombard me, but he doesn't offer anything more. "Are you going to elaborate on that?"

He shakes his head and tips the rest of his beer back, swallowing it down. "Nope, because we're not here to talk about me. We're here to have fun and live in the now. After all, if we're sticking to what you wanted, we would've already had all these getting-to-know-you conversations."

Irritation flares to life instantly. "Well, if you hadn't disappeared three years ago, standing me up and leaving me wondering if you were dead, maybe I would know the answers. But you can't even give me that—the reason you left. I mean, what the hell, Cav? I deserve some sort of explanation." All the bitterness I've been holding on to for three years leaks into my tone like acid.

Cav sets the beer bottle on the table with a *whack*. "Not tonight, Greer."

"Is that another one of your rules? Did I just make it easier for you to avoid answering the question because of my silly little fantasy where we can both pretend you didn't kick me in the gut by leaving?"

His expression shutters, but not before I see pain flash across his features. He doesn't like knowing he hurt me. Well, guess what? I didn't like being hurt, so I figure that makes us even. I've had a lot more time to dwell on it, though.

He presses both elbows to the table and leans toward me. "Are you ever going to be able to let that go? Are you always going to hold it over me?"

I sit back in my chair, crossing my arms. "Would you let it go without some kind of explanation?"

His expression sets into harsh lines when he says, "There are some things you're better off not knowing."

Uncrossing my arms, I reach for my drink and lift it in salute. "Cheers to being so delightfully vague. You should definitely win a medal."

Before Cav can reply, the errant waitress returns with two bottles of water and a tray of food. Conch ceviche and a dozen shrimp and lobster tacos.

The food smells delicious, but my stomach is still knotted. Instead of reaching for the food, I thank her and ask for another drink.

Cav watches me as he piles tacos and ceviche onto his plate. "What would you like?"

"Booze," I reply, my tone as snotty as I've ever heard it.

His eyes narrow. "Am I going to have to fuck this attitude out of you? Because I will. I fucking promise I will."

"All I want is an answer. Some kind of excuse so I can quit thinking about it. You've taken up way too much space in my head for years, and I'm over it. I need to move on with my life." I look up at him. "I need closure."

His mouth set into a thin line, Cav leans forward over the table, pitching his words low so only I can hear them. "You don't need closure because we're not fucking finished, Greer. We're just getting started. Someday I'll give you what you're asking for, but today is not that day. If you're not okay with that, then we're gonna have to find a way to get you okay with it."

Again, delightfully vague, but this time with a hint of a threat.

"Get me okay with it? What does that even mean?" The twisting sensation in my belly fades as hunger takes its place. I reach for a chip and scoop up some ceviche.

An ominous smile pulls at his lips. "I'll fuck you until you can't put two coherent thoughts together, and then I'll take you to the edge over and over, stopping when you're about to come until you're begging me to finally let you. You'll offer me anything I want if I'll just let you have your orgasm." He toys with the neck of his empty beer bottle. "You're a greedy girl when it comes to orgasms, and I'm going to tease you until you think you're going to break."

Heat pools between my thighs, even though part of me wants to toss my water bottle at him. The lack of panties has me intimately aware of the effect of his words.

How can I want him so badly when I still don't trust him? There's nothing stopping Cav from disappearing again. Well, not disappearing completely like he did before, but disappearing from my life.

And if he does? Then what?

I move on once and for all. Fear of losing him slides away because if he walks out like he did before, I'm secure enough in who I am to know that he's not worth wasting my time on. For three years he's been the one who got away, and I was left with too many questions and no answers. But if he leaves again, I'm good. Or at least I will be once I clean up the shards of my shattered heart.

Shattered heart? No, my heart isn't involved in this game. It's sidelined because it can't be objective here. This isn't love; this is lust and closure for the past. I hate lying to myself, but sometimes it's a necessary evil to maintain my sanity and composure.

"And after that?" I ask, a hint of challenge in my voice. "When you can't keep me drunk with pleasure? Am I going to get answers then?"

Cav meets my gaze with his own challenge. "If I think you can handle them."

I reach for my margarita and raise it again in a cheerful salute. "Then let the fucking and orgasm denial begin because I'm not all right with this."

CHAPTER
TWENTY-SIX

Cav

*W*ell, *that didn't go as planned.* I carry a completely hammered Greer from the golf cart through the front door of the house. I didn't expect the first time I carried her over a threshold to be quite like this.

She's nearly incoherent and keeps slipping in and out of consciousness. Trying to keep hold of her during the bumpy golf cart ride is an experience I'd like to avoid in the future. Guilt eats at me because I know I'm the reason for her slamming back three more mango margaritas.

"Greer, we need to get you ready for bed."

"Don't care. Wanna sleep." Her words slur and she sounds so damn young.

Laying her on the bed, I strip off her shirt and pull the skirt down her legs. Her statement earlier about not wearing panties flashes through my brain, along with all the dirty things I want to do to this woman. Things I've wanted to do for years.

But we both know I fucked that up royally tonight. It was on the tip of my tongue to tell her everything, but I couldn't do it. I couldn't watch the sparkle fade from her eyes as she comprehended the truth.

I tuck her into bed and she curls onto her side, facing the windows where the sun will rise so brilliantly in the morning.

Another day with her, and nothing beyond that is guaranteed. I grab her clothes off the floor and lay them on the dresser before venturing into the walk-in closet to find my phone.

Messages from my agent, a director I've been wanting to work with, and . . . Creighton Karas. I knew it wouldn't take him long to track me down. I've got his little sister in my care, and he strikes me as a man who'd kill to protect her.

Well, that makes both of us.

I ignore the messages and shove my phone back into the spot between a pile of men's swim trunks and T-shirts.

I'll protect Greer against any threat that comes her way, but how the hell do I protect her from myself? I'd like to say I'm a good man, but I've never been able to make that claim. For Greer's sake, I wish I could.

How selfish am I going to be? Can I really take what I want without a thought about the cost? That's what I've been doing so far. And that's exactly what I did when I stepped on that jet in LA after Peyton DeLong crowed over the ad.

More than anyone, I know that thoughtless actions have consequences that can cause immeasurable pain. Pain I don't want to cause the woman sleeping only feet from me.

Fuck. I'm going to have to let her go.

The thought is quickly followed by, *Over my dead body.*

CHAPTER
TWENTY-SEVEN

Greer

Toast. That's the only thing I can force down this morning. Let it be known once more that alcohol and I can no longer be friends. I really need to work on that. Even the sweet-smelling freshly cut pineapple seems to mock me from the bowl on the table.

I crunch on the bread and groan. *Why is toast so freaking loud? Shouldn't the traditional morning-after remedy be quieter?* My head pounds, and yet it doesn't force away the memories I have of last night.

I'm so screwed. Does it help to know in advance? I mean, walking into this with my eyes wide open should make it less painful when Cav crushes my heart beneath his Hollywood heel.

No expectations, I tell myself. That's the key. Recalling the deal we made yesterday, I decide it's the only way I can keep myself intact. I'm going to pretend. Pretend I don't care that Cav is keeping secrets from me. Pretend I'm not dangerously close to getting used to having him in my life. Pretend I'm going to be okay when this is all over.

I drop the toast and reach for my orange juice. It's light, sweet, and freshly squeezed, but still I grimace at the acidity in my mouth.

"Are you going to survive?"

Cav's been watching my attempt at enjoying a normal breakfast since I dragged my ass out of bed when the sun was too blindingly bright to keep my eyes closed any longer.

Thank you for the beautiful sunrise, Belize, but let's work on respecting some boundaries.

After taking another sip of my orange juice and replacing it on the table, I answer Cav's question. "I'll survive." Neither of us mentions last night, and I tell myself it's a truce. We're both going to adopt Greer's fantastic pretending plan.

"Anything in particular you'd like to do today?"

When I consider doing anything that requires any sort of sudden movements, my stomach flops in rebellion.

"Nothing exciting. Laying around the pool tops my list."

"Fair enough."

He rises and disappears for a moment before returning with a bottle of ibuprofen. "I should've made you take some last night with more water, but you were out as soon as you hit the bed."

That's a generous assessment. I think I was actually

out before we even made it in the house. Not that it matters, but my morning-after hindsight is incredibly clear.

There's still one question I can't answer. *Am I ever going to be able to get over this nagging feeling of dread?* We have limited time here—presumably until Creighton sends his jet back and demands my presence at home.

That can be at any moment. Am I going to get hung up on things I can't change—at least, not until Cav decides to share whatever he's not telling me? Or am I going to live in the moment and suck this opportunity dry like I promised myself I would?

The latter is my only logical choice.

My hangover gives up around noon, and Rea brings out an enormous cold lobster salad and a fresh baguette.

Cav, I've noticed, eats way more food than any man I've ever met. Probably because he isn't like any other man I've ever met. For the last hour and a half, I've watched him turn this deck and the beach into a gym. Sprints, push-ups, pull-ups on the railing outside, and he even dug up some weights somewhere and used the chaise as a bench. Sweat glistened on his bronzed skin before he finally dived into the pool and began a solid half hour of laps.

Curled up on the chaise, I lower the worn Lisa Kleypas romance novel I found on the shelf inside, finally admitting to myself that although I'm madly in love with the hero of the book, *Blue-Eyed Devil* can't compete with the man in front of me.

No wonder Cav stays so ripped. He works his ass off for it. My eyes lock on his ass, clearly outlined by the board shorts he's wearing as he hauls himself stroke after stroke through the pool.

I've also firmly pushed away reality to focus on the pretend world we're living in. Except for the fact that I'm kicking myself I didn't ask for a continuance on the motion I was drafting for my prisoners' rights case. I know the judge will probably waive the late filing because of the type of case, but I can't bet on it. I know better. I should be better.

One thing I haven't missed since I walked out? The law firm. And yet I don't have a clue what I want to do with my life, although living in paradise seems to be a rising option on my list. If only it could stay like this forever.

But it can't. Life will intrude sooner rather than later.

Cav lifts himself out over the side of the pool, water streaming off his body, muscles flexing and rippling. It's like watching one of his movies up close. He truly does look like he belongs on the big screen. Three years ago, it was obvious he was capable of so much more . . .

"I can't believe I left my keys in that cab! I'm so pissed at myself."

I was standing outside my building near Columbia at midnight. The doorman was MIA, the super wasn't answering his phone, and the streets were deserted. But it was fine. I mean, I was a New Yorker. I was tough. I wasn't scared. But I also didn't want to call my brother and ride uptown to get a spare key.

"Hey, sexy. Lookin' good." A man walked by, checking me out. He slowed a half dozen feet away. "You up for a party tonight?"

I looked down at my clothes. My leather jacket was short and so was my skirt, but the black tights and tall, flat black boots did more than keep my legs warm in the cool night air—they kept me from looking like a hooker.

"I'm waiting for my boyfriend," I told him. "He's right around the corner."

The man eyed me for another beat, mumbled something that sounded like "lying bitch," and resumed his swagger down the street.

I pulled out my phone and hovered over Creighton's number, but I didn't want to be the little sister needing assistance. I was working on proving myself as independent, and this definitely wasn't going to help my case.

My thumb scrolled up a few more numbers to hover over Cav's. He said he lived right around the corner, and something told me he was a night owl like me.

Fuck it. I tapped on his name, thinking a call would probably do me more good than a text.

He answered on the first ring. "What's going on?"

The sound of shouting in the background made me pause before I responded. "Uh, is now a bad time?"

"Hold on one sec." He must have moved away from the source of the noise, because it died after a few moments. "Sorry, there's a fight on in the bar, and people are gettin' rowdy. What can I do for you, baby girl?"

Heat bloomed in my belly and a smile stretched across my face. I loved when he called me that. I'd never understood pet names, but for some reason his made me feel special.

"Are you anywhere near my place?"

"What's wrong?" His tone shifted into high alert.

"I left my keys in a cab on the way home from Tracey's apartment, and it's gone and my doorman is gone and the super is gone and some guy tried to pick me up like I was a hooker. I'm trying not to freak out, but I'm kinda freaking out. I don't want to call my brother. He might still be in China."

"Whoa, calm down, baby. I'm literally across the street—" He paused for a beat. "And I can see you from where I'm standing. You're safe. I'll be there in a second. Don't hang up until you see me."

He can see me? He had to be at Lennon's, the shitty bar that my crowd avoided most nights because there were too many rough-looking regulars who didn't take kindly to students trying to invade their space.

I scanned the street and within moments, Cav appeared beneath a streetlight. Relief swept over me. "I see you."

"Good. Hang up."

I did as he ordered and waited for him to get closer.

"Well, that was convenient," I said with a smile on my face. My moment of panic disappeared as soon as I knew he was near.

Cav shrugged, his canvas jacket unzipped and revealing a black thermal. His jeans were ripped, and his black boots were scuffed. I thought of this as the Cav Uniform because he'd worn something similar every time we'd gone out.

And by every time, I meant the five different "dates" we'd had. An amazing Polish restaurant I hadn't known existed, hot dogs in the park while we walked and talked for hours, playing checkers at a hole-in-the-wall coffee house, and twice watching old movies at a ratty theater where we shared popcorn . . . and a little more. Except he still hadn't rounded third base. Recounting all this in my head made me stop worrying about getting into my apartment and start worrying about whether I was defective on the female front.

"You know I don't live far," he replied.

Yes, I knew this. He'd told me a couple of times, but had been vague on the address and had never invited me over. Actually, he didn't accept any invites into my apartment either, only walking me to my door and disappearing into the night. Yep, I was defective.

"Locked yourself out, eh?" He jerked his chin toward the building.

I rocked back on my heels, my hands in the pockets of my jacket. "I'm an idiot. I was in such a hurry to get out of that cab because the cabbie was skeeving me out—and now my keys are just chilling on the seat." I pulled a hand out of my pocket and pointed at it. "These pockets suck. I lose stuff all the time. Basically, I suck, and it's been a sucky night."

"Where's the guy who talked to you?" Cav's head was turning, searching the dark streets.

"Long gone, hopefully."

Looking back to me, he frowned. "You can't do shit like this, Greer. You're not invincible. You need to stay off these streets after dark."

I narrowly kept from stomping my foot like a toddler since he was scolding me like one. "I know this. I didn't lock myself out on purpose. I don't know where everyone is who's supposed to be able to help."

"Maybe you shouldn't be out late by yourself."

I held up a hand. "Whoa, whoa. I'm twenty-three years old and can do whatever the hell I want. I don't need a babysitter."

"No, but you need a fucking keeper." Cav crowded me into the front of the building. "What if I were looking to get a piece of your fine ass? No one could stop me right now. There's no one around who's gonna save you from me."

I shoved at his chest. "Why the hell aren't you looking to get a piece of my fine ass? I've been wondering when you're finally going to make a move."

His dark scowl faltered with the hint of a smile. "Fuck, you're a sassy thing. Who says I'm not?" The smile faded. "And even if I am, you shouldn't let me. I'm not good enough for you, Greer. You shouldn't let a guy like me get so damn close. It ain't right."

This time, I was the one scowling. "You don't get to decide that for me. Only I get to decide that."

"Because you're twenty-three years old and can do whatever the hell you want," he finished for me.

"Exactly."

A low growl rumbled in his chest, like he wasn't sure what to do with me. He pushed away from the wall and stared up at the building.

"Let's get you inside before daylight, okay?"

"Good. Let's."

"You got a fire escape around the side?"

I jerked a thumb toward the left side of the building. "The one over here comes pretty close to my window."

"Good. Then that's how we're getting in."

"My windows are locked."

Cav's grin flashed. "Not a problem."

He pulled me around the side of the building and stopped under the fire escape. With a single leap, he grabbed the bottom rung and pulled it down. Glancing at me, he said, "You're coming up too."

I looked down at my black boots, glad I'd picked the no-heel pair. "Why?"

"Because I'm guessing you've got one of those fancy alarms that's hooked to your windows, and as soon as I get the fucker open, it's going to start beeping. If you don't put in the code, the cops will be here to arrest me for a B&E."

Shit. I didn't even think about that. I nodded. "Okay."

"You're not scared of heights, are you?"

I shook my head. "No. I'm good. I just don't like climbing fire escapes in a skirt."

"Anyone looks up it, they're gonna answer to me. You go first, and I'll be right below you. You won't fall because I got you, baby girl."

Any lingering fear I had about climbing the fire escape fell away with his reassurance.

"Okay, let's do this."

Ladder after ladder, we climbed to the ninth floor, and I was glad I wasn't living on the seventeenth like I'd originally planned. I stopped at the ninth floor landing when we reached it and leaned over the edge to peer inside my window. My apartment was all locked up nice and tight, without me in it.

Cav pulled me away from the edge of the fire escape. "This is my part. Make sure you hold on. I'm not about to lose you now."

He wasn't even out of breath, and I was huffing and puffing. Apparently Cav didn't skip as many workouts as I did, which explained how damn ripped he was.

"I'm not going to fall off." And he wasn't going to lose me. Shit, he hadn't even had me. Maybe tonight . . . He had to come into the apartment to go back down through the elevator . . .

Quickly, I tried to get my head in seductress mode, which was quite a challenge while the cold night air blew up my skirt. Besides, did I even know how to seduce this guy?

I watched as Cav reached into his pocket and pulled out something, but in the darkness, I couldn't make out what it was. He leaned over the railing of the fire escape to the ledge of my window.

"Shit. Need to get a little closer."

Cav lay down on the fire escape and pulled his body halfway out to the window. He was suspended without support over ninety feet off the ground, and the thought flipped my stomach over into knots. Before I had a chance to ask him what the hell he was doing, he was already shoving the window up and jumping inside my living room.

The beeping of the alarm system came from behind him, just like he'd said it would.

"Come on, baby. I'll help you inside. Come under the railing, and I'll grab you and haul you in."

I ducked down, not wanting to have to explain to the cops why I was breaking into my own place, or how the hell Cav had done it. Seriously, how had he? A lock-pick set?

He reached out from the window and wrapped both hands around my waist. "Trust me?"

I answered honestly. "Yes."

"Bad idea," he murmured before he lifted me off the fire escape, over the gap below and into my place.

"Why would you say—"

"Alarm, Greer. Now."

I glared at him and headed for the panel near my door. When I punched in my code, the beeping stopped.

I wanted answers now. I wasn't even thinking about seduction. But it was all coming together in my head in some disjointed puzzle. Cav was keeping his distance on purpose, and I had no idea why.

I turned back to demand those answers because, fuck it, I was done with this nonsense, but he was speaking quietly into his phone near the window.

When he hung up, he shoved it in his pocket. "I gotta go. You need to track down your keys or get your locks changed. Both would be smarter. Don't know who might've had access to them, and you shouldn't be taking chances."

All this information was processing in my brain, but one piece stuck out. "You have to go? Why?"

"Something came up. I was supposed to be meeting someone at the bar, and they didn't show until now. Wondering where I am."

Claws of jealousy surged within me. "Are you seriously leaving me to go on a date?" I wanted to take the words back as soon as I spoke them, because I didn't really want to hear him say yes.

Cav's deep chuckle filled my ears. "Jealous, baby? Because Rocco ain't exactly got your curves."

Rocco? A guy? My cheeks heated with embarrassment. "Oh."

Cav strode across the room to where I stood dumbly near the alarm panel. Pressing his palms to the wall, he trapped me in his arms. "The fact that you think you could ever have competition shocks the hell out of me."

Grabbing hold of my lady balls, I asked the question that was really on my mind. "Then why haven't you made a move? A real move? What's your problem?"

He dropped one hand from the wall and fingered a lock of my hair. "Because I don't get to have you, and you should know better than to want me to."

I pushed a hand against his chest, over his heart, and the *thud-thud* of it traveled through my palm.

"That's such bullshit, and you know it. You want me. I want you. This is inevitable."

His eyes slid shut and his jaw tensed. "Fuck, I wish it were that simple."

"Why isn't it?"

He stepped away, putting distance between us. "I gotta go. He's waiting for me."

"You didn't answer my question," I said as he moved toward the door. "And that's bullshit."

His head jerked toward me. "Greer, some shit ain't ever gonna make sense to you, and you shouldn't even know people like me. I shouldn't see you again."

My jaw tensed as a crack formed in my heart. This wasn't where I expected tonight to lead. "What? Are you serious? Just like that? I don't understand."

Cav unlocked my dead bolts before yanking the door open. "Good night, Greer."

And then he was gone.

CHAPTER
TWENTY-EIGHT

Cav

"You okay?"

I watch Greer as she stares at me as if she's not actually seeing me. I wonder if she's lost in memories of the past, like the ones that have bombarded me so many times since I showed up at her door.

She shakes her head as if to clear a fog and blinks. "Sorry . . . I was just thinking about things."

"I've been doing quite a bit of that myself." I lower myself to take a seat across the short table from her.

Her eyes widen as if with surprise. "You have?"

I pause as I reach for the glass in front of my plate. "Of course. Then and now. Can't get you off my mind."

Greer's cheeks, already pink from the sun, flush a brighter red.

"Does that surprise you?"

A small nod.

"It shouldn't. You're an unforgettable woman."

As soon as I say it, her lips flatten into a tight line, and I know her well enough now to gauge her thoughts. Whether Greer will voice the question or not, she wants to know why I could possibly leave her if she's so unforgettable.

I wait for her to ask, but she doesn't. She reaches for serving utensils in the lobster salad instead, her mood dimmed.

I'll have to address it eventually. Because with every reminder, I push her further away, even though I can tell she desperately wants to trust me again. But she won't until I can break through. If I could, I would do it with an explanation. But things aren't that simple, and I'm not ready to give up this little bubble we've created by letting reality intrude. I have to find another way.

"What do you want to do today?" I ask, waiting for her to finish piling lobster on her plate before I dig in and serve myself.

"I'm game for anything. I'd love to see more of this place."

"Underwater or on the water?"

Snorkeling and diving are huge draws on this particular island, and we haven't discussed trying either. But there's a boat docked out front, and Juan already offered to take us.

The temporary cloud that fell over Greer fades away with her excitement. "Both? You really want to?"

"Absolutely."

We finish our lunch and carry the dishes inside before I track down Juan. He's raking the sand yard and tossing fallen coconuts over the wall.

"Hey, man. I've got a question for you."

He stops immediately and straightens. "Yes, sir?"

"Snorkeling and a sunset cruise. You think you could make that happen for us this afternoon?"

Juan gives me a decisive nod. "Of course. I fueled the boat yesterday after I went for supplies in San Pedro. I have the perfect place for you both."

"That's great. Greer will love it."

"Okay. Leave in an hour? I'll get the gear."

"Thank you, sir." I hold out my hand for him to shake.

When he does, he says, "My phone has been ringing a lot. I don't answer it anymore, but the messages are getting . . . unhappy."

My jaw clenches because I can only imagine just how unhappy those messages are becoming.

"No need to listen to them. There's nothing you or I want to hear."

"Okay. If you say so."

"Thank you."

I head back to the house, already putting it out of my mind.

CHAPTER
TWENTY-NINE

Greer

"It's a manatee!" My voice sounds like a little kid tearing into a favorite gift at Christmas as I point at the large gray shape in the water.

Juan slows and shuts off the engine. "You want to go swim with it?"

Cav's already anticipating my response. "Up to you, baby."

I grab my mask and snorkel. We've been in and out of the water a half dozen times already, and I'm beginning to tire. But it's a manatee, so hell yeah, I want to get in the water and swim with it.

We've already seen nurse sharks, rays, sea turtles, an octopus, and loads of fish, but a manatee? Just seeing the big gray sea cow reminds me of my class adopting one in kindergarten. Didn't everyone's class do that?

"I'll take that as a *yes*," Cav says as I slip the mask over my head for the seventh time today.

"Take that as a *hell yes*." I slip my feet into my fins and I'm already over the side before I hear Juan's shout of caution.

I'm paddling for all I'm worth when I hear a second splash in the water behind me that must be Cav, but I'm too excited to wait for him. Come on, we're talking a *manatee*. It's only about thirty feet away from me, and I dive under the water to get a better look, making sure to blow through my snorkel to keep the water out.

I mentally *squee* when I realize there are two of them. A mother and a calf float together in the water, and I'm awed by the experience. Seeing them in person is amazing. They're so big and goofy looking and completely endearing.

Knowing I need to keep my distance, I work to stay in place rather than indulge my instinct to keep swimming toward the pair.

A flash of orange appears beside me—Cav's borrowed board shorts. He's a hell of a swimmer, and I've been meaning to ask him all day if he has tried out for roles that were water-based because my guilty Google searches didn't tell me about any.

I flail excitedly, but he doesn't look as amazed by the manatees as I do. Needing to catch my breath, I swim to the surface and blow the salt water from my snorkel tube. Cav's next to me before I'm finished.

Cav pulls his snorkel from his mouth and says, "Come on, baby. We're going back."

I shake my head, pulling my snorkel away as well. "Why? I want to see—"

"Because you're in such a hurry, you didn't wait to hear Juan tell you he just realized there are jellyfish everywhere around here. We need to get you out of the fucking water before you get stung."

"Jellyfish?" Fear paralyzes my limbs, making my head duck under the surface, and I suck in salt water. I thrash to pull myself back up and emerge coughing.

Cav's arm wraps around me and he pulls me against him, keeping my head above water. "You're okay. I got you. I'm not going to let anything happen to you, not even a fucking jellyfish sting. Understand me?"

I nod, wanting to get the hell back in the boat. I didn't know I had an irrational fear of jellyfish, but it's really freaking clear now that I do.

"Good. Juan is coming toward us, and you only have to swim a little farther."

"Okay. Okay. Let's go."

I swim toward the boat, caught between wanting to be careful while making sure I'm not going to tangle with some barely visible monster with tentacles, and getting there as fast as humanly possible. I go for option two.

We get to the side of the boat as Juan shuts down the motor and Cav lifts me up and over the edge. Sometimes his strength still blows my mind, and right now I'm really, really grateful for it. Once I'm back in the boat, Cav climbs in beside me.

I reach for my beach towel, intent on wrapping it around me and forgetting this whole experience, except for the manatees, but Cav snatches it from my hands.

"I need to check you for stings. Did you feel anything? Did they get you?"

Confusion reigns as I shake my head. "No, I didn't feel anything."

He gets to his knees in front of me, checking my legs and torso before lifting me to my feet and turning me around. Only once he's satisfied that I escaped the jellyfish without incident does he wrap the towel around me.

"Fuck, you scared the shit out of me, Greer."

"I'm sorry. I didn't hear him and I wanted to see . . ." My words trail off as I see two red spots on his calf. "They got you? Holy shit. Oh my God, Cav. I'm so sorry!" I turn to Juan. "What do we do? How do we treat it? Do we need something special? Do you need to pee on him?"

Cav spins me around in the rocking boat and presses a kiss to my forehead. "Shh. Calm down."

Juan comes over and squats down to look at Cav's leg. "Tentacles didn't stick. Just barely stung you. Let me get a bucket of seawater and you can rinse. Should only sting for a few minutes and you'll be good."

I'm feeling all the guilt as Cav does as Juan's instructed. "I'm so sorry. I got too excited."

Cav grabs my hand. "Hey. Stop. Baby, I'm fine. It doesn't even hurt. Just a little sting and an itch. It's already fading."

"But—"

He squeezes my fingers. "I'd take a bullet for you, Greer. This is nothing."

He's smiling, but I'm trying to comprehend what he

just said. *I'd take a bullet for you.* He means every word, and it's the most powerful thing anyone has ever said to me. My iron-clad grip on my heart loosens by degrees.

"I don't want you getting hurt for me," I say quietly.

"That's not something you get to choose." He lowers himself onto the cushioned bench seat in front of the cockpit and pulls me down beside him.

I'm quiet the rest of the boat ride to the island, having lost my appetite for adventure for the moment. Cav picks up on my changing mood.

"You okay?" he asks over the roar of the engine and the hull slapping the Caribbean blue water as we head toward the channel that will let Juan back in through the reef.

"Yeah. Just . . ." I let my words trail off because I have no idea what to say.

"Still freaking out?"

I meet his hazel gaze. "Yeah. I don't like that feeling. At all."

Cav's arm tightens around my shoulders. "Everything's fine."

"It's not fine. You got hurt because of me. Because I didn't wait and listen."

"Don't beat yourself up. If you take this as a reminder to look before you leap, then we're good."

I force a smile to my lips. "I guess I need to do that more often, huh?"

One of Cav's eyebrows hitches up. "It wouldn't hurt. But luckily, you've got me to catch you when you make those jumps. I won't let you fall."

Do I really have him? Maybe for now, in this fantasy bubble. But what about when this is over? I'm waiting for a message from Creighton that the coast is clear and all the concerns have been contained.

What happens when we're back in the real world? Do Cav and I have a future? Those are the questions I should be asking, but I'm not ready to hear the answers yet.

Instead, I lean into his heat and watch the beginnings of a beautiful sunset paint the sky.

CHAPTER THIRTY

Cav

Every day we're here, I'm more and more fucked. Spending so much time with Greer has done nothing but reaffirm the fact that leaving her three years ago, while inevitable, is the worst decision I've ever made. After we got back to the house following the jellyfish incident, she fussed over me, wishing she could google how to properly treat it. Juan gave us some pointers, but still Greer worried.

She fucking worried about me.

I haven't had someone worry about me . . . in a long time.

That fact just brings it home that Greer is one of a kind. I've been wanted for my fame, my notoriety, and my money, but with Greer, I know it's none of those things.

She's the billionaire's sister who wanted the mainte-nance man. A fact that still blows me away and reminds me how much time I wasted.

Buttoning a light cotton shirt, I walk to the doorway of the bathroom where she's putting on makeup in front of the mirror. She's fucking beautiful. And she could already be mine if I wasn't who I am.

Hollywood and the movie business gave me the chance to flip the bird to the reasons that kept us apart, and this time I'm not letting her go, regardless of what comes next. I'm going to make this real.

"I'm almost ready, I swear," Greer says, meeting my eyes in the mirror.

"Take your time. We're in no hurry. And you know you don't need to get all dolled up to eat dinner on the deck, right?"

Her glare is too cute not to smirk at.

"I'm not sitting across from you—looking all drop-dead gorgeous—without looking equally sexy. Or at least as sexy as I can manage. It's called balance, Cavanaugh. Deal with it."

I think it's the first time she has called me by my full name, and my brain skips forward to some vision of the future where she's telling me to suck it up and deal with her primping for the red carpet premiere of one of my movies.

Fuck, having her on my arm for that would be a dream. Every time I've stepped in front of the flashing cameras for a premiere, I've wondered if she'd see the pictures. I wanted her to see the pictures. I wanted her to wish she was with me instead of that fuck Tristan.

And now she is.

Taking one last long look at her as she does something to make her eyes look even deeper and darker, I turn to wander the house. If I keep watching her, I'll bend her over the bathroom counter, tell her to keep her hands on the mirror and her eyes on mine as I bury myself inside her.

Soon.

I make my way through the living room, loving how fucking untouchable we are here. The outside world can't break into our bubble. Rea and Juan have followed my instructions from the first day impeccably—that we not be bothered with any calls they might receive—in exchange for a healthy tip to express my gratitude.

A table is already set up on the patio, a candle flickering on the white tablecloth between two plates. I can hear Rea in the kitchen, finishing up dinner preparations.

Snapper, shrimp, and lobster with coconut rice and vegetables. Fresh pineapple-coconut ice cream for dessert, all at Greer's request.

"Mmm . . . that smells delicious."

I turn to see Greer behind me, her borrowed purple dress hitting high on her thighs, her dark hair wild around her shoulders. *Greer undone*—that's the look she has right now, and it's completely at odds with the smooth sophistication she exuded in New York. Both are sexy, but this is more . . . real.

"Are you ready to be served?" Rea asks.

"We are, thank you. Would you like a hand?"

"No, sir. I have it all ready."

Greer weaves her fingers through mine and together

we walk toward the table. The ocean is dark, and the only light on the patio comes from the candle on the table and the glow of iron fixtures attached to the cement walls of the house.

"Romantic," she whispers.

"Rea did a hell of a job." And from the aroma wafting off the plates she's carrying behind us, she knocked dinner out of the park as well. She sets them on the table as I pull out Greer's chair for her.

"Everything look good?"

"It looks amazing," Greer replies. "Thank you."

"I'll bring the wine, and then I'll leave you two alone." She bustles away as I seat myself across from Greer.

When Rea returns with the bottle and departs with a smile, we unwrap the cloth napkins from around our silverware and dig into the meal.

Greer's moaning with pleasure over the lobster, and I want her moaning like that on my cock.

Soon. She has no idea what she's in for. Tonight, I'm going to show her exactly what it means to be mine.

CHAPTER
THIRTY-ONE

Greer

All day, I've been wishing I could call Banner and beg for advice. My best friend would get my head on straight. I asked Cav if we could pretend that this was real, that we were an *us*, and I got the tropical island fantasy version of it.

So, why am I panicking now? Because pretending this is real is pulling me down a path that terrifies me. This was supposed to be a fling, and then I had to go and change the rules, putting my heart in jeopardy.

I've always struggled to be a *live in the moment* kind of girl. My brain doesn't stop at *oh, today is a great day, I should enjoy this.* No, I'm always thinking about what happens next. And for me and Cav, what's next is a gray and murky space.

Without cell service or Wi-Fi, I can't throw this problem at Banner and get her slightly crass but *real* advice. WWBD. What would Banner do? I can hear her voice in my head.

He's hot as shit, Greer. Fuck the hell out of the guy. Get as many orgasms as you can and save those memories for a rainy day with your vibrator. And make sure to give me all the dirty details. But whatever you do, don't let your heart get involved, you silly little sap.

The voice is right. I need to take everything I can from this moment and hold the memories close like I did the ones from three years ago. Ride the high, but fortify the walls of my heart to protect against the inevitable crash.

The entire time my mind is furiously working at problem solving, I'm also caught up with staring at Cav.

Never in a million years could I have anticipated that we'd be having a candlelit dinner with the sound of the ocean waves crashing on the beach only feet away. Even my fantasies are never this creative.

Several minutes have passed since the last word of conversation, and he's staring at me as well.

"Your dinner okay?"

I look down at my plate, which I've nearly cleared already.

"Amazing. I could eat like this every day. It's easy to get spoiled by the food here."

"It's easy to get spoiled by a lot of things here," he replies. "Especially having you naked in my arms every night."

I shiver at the memories of Cav waking me up in the most decadent ways. Losing sleep in the middle of the night isn't a concern when orgasms are a guarantee.

It also makes me want to heed the advice I think Banner would give.

"I've gotten spoiled by that too. And the orgasms. You make me greedy."

Cav's hazel eyes are golden-green tonight, and at my words, they take on an intense light that's becoming familiar.

"Your ice cream is going to have to wait because I want my dessert first." He stands and picks up both our empty plates. "Get up here. I want your legs spread so I can eat that pretty pussy."

Blinking at how quickly Cav stole control of this moment and changed gears, I find myself standing and then coming around to his side as he clears the rest of the dishes.

When he returns from inside and the fastest dinner cleanup I've ever seen, I'm still not sitting on the table like he ordered.

"You must want me to remind you what I do to bad girls who don't follow the orders I give them." The deep, forbidding tone of Cav's voice promises that I'm going to love what he's planning. "Bend over the table and lift up your dress."

Shivers ripple through me, and they have nothing to do with the breeze coming off the ocean.

My logical mind fights the order for a second too long. Cav reaches out, his hands gripping me around the waist, and pulls me where he wants me. One hand fists my hair and the other presses against the small of my back until my chest connects with the tablecloth.

"You like when I put you where I want you, don't you, baby girl?"

"I don't know," I whisper, my fingers curling around the opposite edge of the table.

"Don't lie to me or yourself," he says, his voice low as he flips up the skirt of my dress. "It's just going to make your punishment last longer."

"Is it really punishment if I like it?" I have no idea where the devil inside me came from who uttered that question.

Cav turns my head to the side so I can see his face. His expression is wicked. "You're my bad, dirty girl." His other hand moves from the small of my back down to the bare skin of my ass. "And tonight I'm going to show you just how dirty you were made to be."

His eyes gleam as he releases his grip on my hair and lands a strike on my left cheek. The burning sting that I've become well acquainted with under Cav's hand warms my skin, and heat builds between my legs.

Three more sharp smacks come before he stops.

"Spread your legs," he orders.

I follow his command, uncaring who could see the depraved sight of me bent over the table, Cav turning my ass red.

"Finally, my dirty girl is following orders. Almost makes me feel guilty that I'm going to do this."

As my mind struggles to keep up with his words, a whoosh of cold air rushes toward my clit and Cav's palm connects.

"Ahhh!" I jerk against the table, but I'm pinned in place by Cav's hand in my hair and I can't move any further.

When his hand comes back, I tense, but instead of delivering another strike, he cups my pussy.

"When I tell you I want your ass on the table and legs spread so I can eat this cunt, the only question you should be asking is *how wide*. Understand me, baby girl?"

His expression dares me to contradict him, followed by a smirk of triumph. He can feel the wetness his filthy words produce dripping onto his palm.

Dammit. How can I protest something he knows turns me into a panting mess?

Cav's thick fingers stroke my clit, and my hips press against them, wanting more pressure. More everything. Without warning, he pulls back and delivers another slap to my clit.

This time it's my moan echoing across the water, and I'm shameless because I don't care who hears me.

He circles my clit with one blunt fingertip. "Now, what exactly am I going to do with you tonight? Fuck your face? Pound into your pussy so you're still feeling me when we sit down for dinner tomorrow night?"

The daring devil inside me speaks before thinking. "Yes. All of it."

His thumb slides back toward my ass. "And this. You're ready for a hard cock up this tight little ass."

Heat zings from my hard nipples to my clit, and I'm equal parts terrified and excited.

Bold, Greer. Grab every moment you can.

"Yes. To everything."

Cav's groan is gratifying, but I miss his fingers as soon as he moves them away.

"Wha—" The question on my lips is cut off as he pulls me off the table to a standing position, only to pick me up once again and sit my ass on it.

"Wide."

One word. One order. That's all it takes for my body to respond to him in ways it has never responded to another man.

I'm so screwed. But at least I'm going to enjoy it.

I spread my legs like the shameless dirty girl he calls me as Cav lowers himself to his knees and grips each of my inner thighs with a palm.

"Fucking beautiful. I love the taste of this sweet pussy." And he devours me.

Some men only pretend to love to eat pussy, but Cav is the real deal. Lips, teeth, and tongue—he uses them all to bring me to the edge. I clutch his head with both hands, as though I'm afraid he's going to try to move before I can grab the orgasm hovering just out of reach.

But he doesn't disappoint. Cav never does when it comes to my pleasure. A fingertip teases my opening before pushing inside and stroking forward, hitting *that spot*.

"I'm—ah—"

He growls against my clit, and the vibrations coupled with the pressure on my G-spot take me where I need to be. My orgasm beats through me faster and more intense than the crash of the waves on the shore.

I release my grip on his head and fall forward, catching myself on his shoulders.

Cav pulls back. "Fuck, I love how responsive you are. Every time, you just throw yourself into it without holding back."

Releasing my inner thighs, he begins to rise. Before I know what he's planning, his shoulder presses to my stomach and he tosses me up and over it. My dress flies up, and Cav steadies me with a hand on my bare ass.

"We're moving this party to the bedroom. No more free shows."

CHAPTER
THIRTY-TWO

Cav

I toss Greer onto the bed and her body splays on the white coverlet crossways. Supplies I gathered earlier are in the nightstand. Rope. Lube. Black blindfold. I pull them out of the drawer and set them on the top.

I've never been ashamed of my kinks, but for all these years I've wondered how Greer would react to them. The verdict is in—she's fucking perfect. Right down to the way her eyes widen at the sight of the rope.

"What are you doing with that?"

"No questions. Yellow to slow down and red to stop. You understand?"

I study her reaction carefully, pleased when her pupils dilate and her skin flushes pink. I curl a hand into the skirt of her dress and drag it up her body.

"Arms up."

Greer doesn't hesitate, following directions like she was born to. My cock hardens further at the sight of her naked skin.

"No panties and no bra? You really are a dirty girl."

She opens her mouth to say something, but closes it again.

"You can speak, baby. You just don't get to question what I'm going to do with you."

A mischievous smile tugs at her lips. "I wanted you to have easy access."

"I always knew you were a brilliant woman."

Her cheeks flush a deeper pink at my compliment, and I want to see that color painting her whole body.

I snag the rope and uncoil it. It's not exactly up to my normal standards, but it'll work. I want her to know exactly how it feels to be bound and at my mercy.

Moving around the bed, I bring her wrists together and wrap the soft rope around them, binding them and leaving a long tail wrapped around the center between her hands, which I use to tie off on the bed frame. She has enough give to move some, but not far, and by design, I can flip her from front to back without putting more tension on her bindings.

A scan of her face reveals a wide, anxious gaze. Lower, her nipples are hardened into perfect points. Her legs arch over the edge of the bed, ready for me to step between them and take her.

"You look beautiful bound for me. How do you feel?"

Her pink flush travels from her cheeks down her chest, and I follow the path with my fingertips, watching her shiver while I wait for her to answer.

"Excited. Nervous. I think?"

"Nervous because I can do anything I want to you? Excited because I'm going to make you come harder than you've ever come before?"

"Yes," she whispers.

"Smart girl."

CHAPTER
THIRTY-THREE

Greer

I'm laid out and tied up like a sacrifice on this bed. I've never felt more exposed and vulnerable, but also strangely powerful. Cav's eyes never leave mine as he unfastens one button at a time and his shirt floats to the floor.

I drink him in—broad shoulders, hard pecs, defined abs, flexing biceps, and forearms leading to hands I want on my body. His dark hair is mussed and his hazel eyes are still golden-green in this light—and riveted on me.

No man has ever made me feel this sexy. Tonight, there are no boundaries. Nothing is off-limits. I want him to take everything he wants from me because I'm dying for it too.

Cav's hands go to the button of his khaki shorts and he shoves them down his hips. His thick cock springs free and I bite my lip, wanting it in my mouth. He brought me to the edge of madness on the table, and I want to return the favor. This isn't a power struggle; it's a pleasure struggle. A battle to see who can give more than they take.

He fists his cock, stroking the shaft. "I'm going to fuck your face while you're bound and helpless."

A flood of heat blooms between my legs. How can words make me so wet? He rounds the bed, coming toward my head, and my mind is skipping through possibilities, trying to picture what he's thinking. Luckily, I don't need to wait long.

"Turn over, up on your knees." Cav grasps my shoulders and helps steady me. "Forearms on the bed. Chin up."

I follow each order until I'm staring down the length of his cock, my mouth watering to suck the head of it inside.

Cav must read the need on my face because he grips his cock again and paints the crown over my lips. "Lick."

My tongue comes out and swirls around before I close my lips around his cock. Cav pulls back, the head leaving my mouth with a *pop*. My gaze cuts to his.

"I said lick. Not suck." His hand taps my cheek before cupping it. "This is about what I want. And I want to watch you lick my cock before I make you take it all."

Something about his words, knowing that he's taking what he wants from me, makes this exponentially hotter.

He comes closer and I lick, keeping my eyes locked on his. The satisfied smile curving his mouth makes me want to beg to take everything he's promising.

"Now suck. Wrap those lips around my cock and take it in. I want it nice and slick so I can fuck your face, baby girl."

My nipples stiffen further, almost to the point of pain. I didn't know it was possible to be this turned on just from sucking dick, but the wetness between my legs is slicking down my inner thighs.

"Good girl. Now it's my turn." Cav cradles my jaw as he begins to thrust. "Keep your eyes on me. I want to watch them get big and wide when you feel how deep you can take me."

I breathe through my nose as he presses forward, and suck as he withdraws.

His cock sinks deeper and deeper with every stroke until he bumps the back of my throat and his hand tangles in my hair. "Swallow me down. I want to feel it."

I keep my breaths even as I swallow on the next stroke. Tears gather in my eyes and spill down my cheeks, but I do it. I've got his cock in my throat, and the approval glowing in his eyes urges me to take more on the next stroke.

"Fucking perfect," Cav says as he pulls his cock free of my mouth.

"But—"

"I'm not coming down your throat, Greer. I'm not coming at all until I'm buried in your ass."

Shivers ripple along my skin at his determination and conviction. I'm losing my last shred of innocence tonight, and I'm glad it's with him. I feel like I saved something for him that no other man will ever have.

"Forehead on the bed, ass in the air, and spread your legs. I want to see that sweet pink cunt before I fuck it."

Again, I feel every bit the dirty girl he calls me as I

follow his instructions. Tied to the edge of the bed, my eyes closed and my legs spread, I have no secrets from this man. I hear the pop of a cap, but don't understand the sound until Cav kneels behind me on the bed and I feel slickness sliding between my ass cheeks.

Wait. He's going straight for—?

Pressure against my back entrance registers before I can think any further. A finger. No, the pad of his thumb. Not the thick head of his cock, because that's pressing against my pussy.

"I'm going to fill both your holes and stretch out this asshole for my cock. I can't wait to have a plug for you so I can fuck you with it filled every time. You'll scream for me. And then I'll fuck your ass while I've got a vibrator buried in your pussy, and make you come until you pass out from the pleasure."

He doesn't scare me—he thrills me. I want it. I can't wait to experience all the dirty, filthy things he wants to do to me.

"Press back. You're going to help me fill this ass and stretch it out."

I hesitate, and a stinging smack lands on the outside of my left hip.

"Now, baby girl. Show me what a sweet little slut you're going to be for me and only me."

I press backward at his urging, and his thumb breaches the sensitive ring of muscle until it slips inside. My nerve endings zing with sensation, and my pussy drips at the fullness. I need him inside me.

Cav reads my mind and shoves forward with a single

thrust, burying his cock to the hilt.

I cry out something incomprehensible as he withdraws and thrusts again. Over and over he fucks into me, his thumb taking my ass on counterstrokes. I brace my arms against the bed to absorb the power in his movements. I'm flying toward the edge of an orgasm when one arm wraps around my hip and a sharp smack lands against my clit.

Detonation.

"Cav!" I yell his name as the orgasm tears through me, gripping the rope binding me to the bed because I need some kind of anchor.

He continues for several more thrusts before stopping and pulling free.

"Fuck, baby, I'm so goddamn close, but I'm not letting go yet."

His thumb slides free and I hear the sound of the cap again. "I'm going to go slow. I fucking promise. You've got yellow and red if you need them."

Cav coats my asshole with the slick oil, and the head of his cock presses against my opening. "I know I'm a hell of a lot bigger than my thumb, but you can take me." With one hand on my ass, he strokes and teases my clit with the other.

Pressure. Pressure. A sizzle of dark pleasure. I've never felt so unbelievably *full* before as he breaches the ring of muscle with the head of his cock. The same sensations slip through me as when he used his thumb, but they're multiplied a thousandfold because he's so damn big. A razor-thin edge of pain wraps through the pleasure, but I've never wanted this more.

"I'm in your ass, baby. Fuck, you look so beautiful taking my cock. Sexiest fucking thing I've ever seen in my life."

The pressure increases on my clit and slickness drips through his fingers, but I don't care as he goes deeper. Finally, I feel the press of his hips against my ass. He's in. All the way. And he feels huge, but . . . strangely perfect.

"Hold on, baby girl, it's time to take your man. Fuck, I've been waiting years to feel this. It was worth every second of the wait. Sweet fucking girl. Dirty beautiful girl. All mine."

He pulls back, never stopping with the pressure on my clit. When he's nearly all the way out, he presses in again, and the dance of sweet pain and dark pleasure begins anew. It's mind-bending. I don't know how to comprehend all the sensations rioting in my brain.

An acute sense of possession and ownership pervades it all. I feel shameless. Naughty. Dirty. And I love every single second of it.

Soon, I'm pressing back as he thrusts forward; we're working in time and I'm hovering on the brink of another orgasm. It's so close, and all I have to do is reach for it.

"Fuck, baby girl. I'm gonna fuck your ass harder and you're going to come for me, and when you do, you're gonna scream."

His strokes increase in pace and my fingers claw at the sheets, desperate for some hold. My sanity is fading away at the edges as pleasure and need and desire for Cav cloud my brain.

"I'm so close." My voice breaks on the words.

"When I say."

"Please," I beg. "I need—"

"Fucking come for me and squeeze my cock."

Two more strokes, another slap to my pussy, and I'm soaring. Splintering apart. Shattering into pieces.

Cav's roar fills my ears and heat pumps into my ass as he comes.

I'm murmuring incoherently when he finally slows his movements. He falls forward, bracing himself above me while my body trembles with aftershocks of the mind-blowing orgasm.

Check yes, please *next to the "more back door" box.*

My arms wobble, losing the strength to hold me up.

Cav presses a kiss to my shoulder, the back of my neck, and then my hair.

"Let me take care of this and I'll clean you up."

He pulls out and I want to help, but I'm bound. It doesn't matter, though, because Cav has it covered. I hear water in the bathroom. Within a few moments, he cleans me up with a warm, damp washcloth and comes around the bed to untie my hands.

He helps me off the bed and lifts me into his arms, carrying me into the shower, which is already filling with steam.

"Let's get you cleaned up, baby."

I turn myself over to his care, feeling not only taken by him but *cherished* as he washes me and then wraps me in a towel. Exhaustion is tugging at my eyelids, and there's nothing I want to do more than fall asleep in his arms.

Cav tucks me into bed, and I'm already out before he wraps his body around mine.

CHAPTER
THIRTY-FOUR

Cav

The brilliant morning sun beats in through the window, but that's not what wakes me.

It's the deep voice roaring through the house.

"Where the fuck is she?" the voice demands.

Juan must be trying to preserve our privacy, because he's arguing with someone. "Mr. Karas, I'm sorry, but you need to wait—"

"No fucking way. Where are they?"

Fuck.

My time is up. Our bubble is about to undergo the equivalent of a nuclear holocaust, and Creighton Karas may just try to kill me.

I will not bend to him. I may not be a billionaire, but I'm a long way from being without my own reserves of money and power.

Greer sits up, hair mussed, eyes blinking. "What the hell? Is that my brother?"

"Yes."

I wrap a hand around her shoulder and barely stop myself from shaking her. I need to lay all my cards out on the table, but I don't have enough time to do it justice. All I can say is the one thing that might make a difference.

"Whatever he says to you, you need to know that I'm in love with you, Greer. That's all that matters."

"What did you say?" she asks, her eyes widening with shock, her tone disbelieving.

"I love you. You're mine. And not even Creighton Fucking Karas is going to keep us apart."

Vehemence coats my every word, and I hope she's ready for what's coming next. I reach over and grab my shorts off the floor. I'm buttoning them when the bedroom door flies open and Creighton Karas stalks in.

I snag Greer's dress and toss it to her on the bed before turning to face Karas.

"Get the hell out of here until your sister has a chance to get dressed."

"Don't fucking talk to me like that, boy. You're gone. Done. One-way ticket back to Hollywood and out of her life."

"Crey, what the hell are you doing here?" Greer asks as she tugs the dress over her sheet-covered body. "You were so not invited on this trip, and it was your idea that we lay low, so we're laying low. You can't storm in here and start yelling like a crazy person."

"That was before I knew who he really was." Karas

looks from his sister to me, and then he starts dropping the bombs. "You've been following her for years."

"It's not what it seems like, Crey. I knew him before and—"

"Because he was assigned to follow you. Not get close to you, just fucking follow you."

My eyes are on Greer and the confusion branding her features.

"What?" Her voice is barely audible.

Karas speaks again, but I never take my gaze off her. "Three years ago, you were a job, Greer. His fucking job for the family. He's one of the men Dominic Casso had protecting you without our knowledge."

Confusion turns to understanding as the pieces click together in her clever brain. "The mob? That family?"

My entire body tenses as I wait for her full reaction.

"Yes, the mob." Karas takes another step closer. "He's done nothing but lie to you since the first day you met him."

"That's a fucking lie in itself." My tone comes out just as strong as his.

Karas's eyes are hard. "Fuck if it isn't. Why don't you tell her your real name, Cav. Because it sure as hell isn't Cavanaugh Westman."

A sound escapes from Greer's lips, and my attention jumps back to her.

"What?" All the happiness and easiness that had become her second nature in this house evaporate, leaving her looking shattered.

There's nothing I can do now but admit the truth. "My

name is Cavanaugh Casso."

"Does that mean—" Greer's too fucking quick for her own good, and her brother—her half brother, if we're going to be accurate, because Greer and Creighton only share a mother—is all too happy to deliver the final blow to the trust we've regained.

"He's my fucking half brother. Dominic Casso is his father and mine."

GREER AND CAV'S STORY CONCLUDES IN DIRTY LOVE.

Also by Meghan March

Author's Note

I'd love to hear from you. Connect with me at:

UNAPOLOGETICALLY SEXY ROMANCE

Website: www.meghanmarch.com

Facebook: www.facebook.com/MeghanMarchAuthor

Twitter: www.twitter.com/meghan_march

Instagram: www.instagram.com/meghanmarch

ABOUT

THE AUTHOR

Meghan March has been known to wear camo face paint and tromp around in the woods wearing mud-covered boots, all while sporting a perfect manicure. She's also impulsive, easily entertained, and absolutely unapologetic about the fact that she loves to read and write smut.

Her past lives include slinging auto parts, selling lingerie, making custom jewelry, and practicing corporate law. Writing books about dirty-talking alpha males and the strong, sassy women who bring them to their knees is by far the most fabulous job she's ever had.

She loves hearing from her readers at:

meghanmarchbooks@gmail.com

Made in the USA
San Bernardino, CA
10 June 2016